DIASPORIC

Traditional Chinese cuisine, jade, batik, embroidery, and horticulture.

In Soon Ai Ling's fiction, newly translated into English by Yeo Wei Wei, the lives of twentieth-century Chinese diaspora unravel in the midst of emblems and environments resplendent with cultural influences from East and Southeast Asia.

Life is strange, painful, and beautiful. In stories set across Singapore, Hong Kong and Malaysia, the characters in *Diasporic* struggle for freedom to love, freedom from fate.

A multi-generational family mourns the mysterious disappearance of a flamboyant uncle with vampiric complexion. A teacher looks forward to her reunion with an apprentice whom she has adored for decades and secretly worships as a reincarnated goddess of Chinese embroidery. A teenager tries to save her baby by hugging a vending machine and refusing to give birth.

DIASPORIC

SHORT STORIES BY
SOON AI LING

Translated from the Chinese by

Yeo Wei Wei

BALESTIER PRESS
LONDON · SINGAPORE

Balestier Press
Centurion House, London TW18 4AX
www.balestier.com

Diasporic: Short Stories by Soon Ai Ling
Translated by Yeo Wei Wei

Chef Tham (谭家师傅); *Fans of the Phoenix* (凤凰迷);
Jade and Fate (玉无缘); *Clove* (羽丁香); *Batik Melody* (斑布曲);
Bai Xiangzu and Her Embroidered Peacocks (白香祖与孔雀图);
Jade Butterflies (玉魂扣); *The Song of Life* (生之曲);
Blossoms of the Moon Season (月季花):

First published by Balestier Press in 2023

A CIP catalogue record for this book is available from the British Library.

ISBN 978 1 913891 38 1

Cover design by Sarah and Schooling

This book is a work of fiction. The literary perceptions and
insights are based on experience, all names, characters, places,
and incidents either are products of the author's imagination
or are used fictitiously.

CONTENTS

如果离散是上个世纪的历史印记，那其实是生存的年轮和生活的足迹。

小说的主角们带有个人的执着和倔强，不轻易的妥协，不随意的放弃。因此前面一汪海洋，或一片土地，无论向前或止步，或停留，都会看着四周的环境，身边的家人，对你关心和不关心的人，其实都是深思熟虑，到头来不得不如此。每一个自己是多么的重要，可是离散很多的时候，会问自己你能付出的是多少，而不是你想得到的是什么。

If diaspora is a historical imprint of the last century, it is actually a mark of survival and a footprint of life.

The protagonists in the these stories exemplify conviction and perseverance, refusing to compromise or give up. Whether facing a vast ocean or a swathe of land, whether moving forward or standing still, remaining still, they survey their surroundings, they consider the people around them, their family members, the ones who love and don't love them. All this is undertaken carefully, for this is the only way. The self is to be cherished, and yet a lot of times, the dilemma faced by the diasporic self has to do with how much he or she is willing to sacrifice, rather than what he or she can gain.

孙爱玲
Soon Ai Ling

CHEF THAM

C HEF THAM didn't begin his career in our family kitchen, nor was Tham his actual surname. Before he joined us, he was the head chef of the Tham family. How he came to work for us is a complicated tale.

This story begins at the time when Guangzhou was under the sway of the Cohong, the guild of merchants who controlled China's trade with the west. The most powerful families were the Pans, the Thams and the Wus. The Cohong ran the Thirteen Factories, a neighbourhood of warehouses which the European merchants, known as Tai-Pans, used as their base. Goods and wares between China and Europe were bought and sold in the Thirteen Factories. Tea and silk were exported from China, whilst the Tai-Pans brought guns, gunpowder, western medicines, sculptures and furniture into China.

The Thams and our family were the Cohong's Jiangnan and Jiangbei representatives, north and south of the Yangtze River. We aggregated goods and produce at these points and distributed them to Guangzhou. The Tai-Pans exported Chinese spices and tea to Europe. The Thams were spice merchants, our family, tea. Our business ties made us close. According to Sister Liu, back then, whenever one of the families in the Cohong hosted a banquet, it was fine for the heads of the families to attend without their concubines but not without their chefs.

The chefs who made it to the kitchens of these families were the best chefs in China. Some even came down from the capital in the north, no doubt lured by the large salaries only the Cohong families could pay. Chef Tham's hometown was in Zhejiang, and he specialised in Hangzhou cuisine. It was said that when he moved south, he brought with him an apprentice with legendary knife skills and a cornucopia of kitchenware.

Sister Liu used to accompany Grandfather and Second Grandmother to the Thams' banquets. According to Sister Liu, the Thams served their Dong Bo pork belly differently from us. They didn't bring it out on a platter, but in blue and white porcelain soup bowls, one for each guest. These bowls were tightly lidded. The bowl was the sort of vessel that is still used today for making double-boiled soups. The insulation of these soup bowls meant that the pork belly was steaming hot when it was scooped out with a spoon. What concerned us the most was the taste, whether if the pork belly was delicious, and according to Sister Liu, the meat tasted good because it had been marinaded with Huatiao wine.

Chef Tham was a prized chef. So why did he decide to leave the Thams? How did he come to cook for us? The Tham family business was in the import of pepper, cloves and nutmeg from the Western Yunnan border with Indo-China. The dissolution of the Cohong meant the end of their trade, and all the families had to find a different way to do business. The Thams made use of their Siamese connections to trade in teak, and so their entire family had to move to Thailand. Some of the families had started to sell guns and gunpowder, which was seen as another reason for the rest to be decisive about their next move. Apart from his mother, Chef Tham had a wife and young children. He decided that he wouldn't follow the Tham family on their long journey to Thailand. Through Old Master Tham, Chef Tham sought to come and work for us, saying that he was prepared to be Second Chef in the kitchen.

Grandfather was naturally delighted by this turn of events. It had long been a secret wish of his to hire a chef who specialised in Zhejiang cuisine. Chef Tham as Second Chef? Out of the question! The current political climate worried Grandfather and besides, he'd been thinking that it was about time he retired to his hometown. The political situation was chaotic and worsening by the day. Grandfather decided to close shop and arranged for Second Grandmother, Sister Liu and Chef Tham and his family to move back to the countryside whilst he and Uncle Ding stayed behind in Guangzhou to take care of family residence, our tea shop and other business matters.

Chef Tham was accompanied by his mother, his wife, his apprentices and their families. Together with the high-born Second Grandmother and the petite and pretty Sister Liu, they made the journey by slow boat down the Longjiang River to Huiyang.

From then on, Chef Tham joined our family. The fine dishes he cooked turned all of us, from eldest to the youngest members in the family, all the young masters and misses, into gourmands. He was a virtuosic chef who often added twists to his dishes. Well-versed in the cuisines of the north and the south, his braised pig trotters were rendered in the southern style rather than the northern. The marinade in which he steeped the trotters was a blend of soy sauces, salt, sugar, cooking wine, and afterwards he browned them in a wok with a bit of oil before brushing two smashed cubes of fermented beancurd over them, finally adding water and braising them for four hours. The meat was so tender it slipped off the bones, and the gravy was thick and fragrant. At dinner time, with everyone seated around the table after they finished their soups, Chef Tham brought the braised pig trotters out in deep bowls. With chopsticks and a bamboo knife, he flicked the meat deftly off the bones and when he was satisfied that there wasn't a shred of meat left, he said, 'Please,' and we raised our chopsticks and chimed in unison: 'Thank you, Chef!' The moment a morsel of that meat entered your mouth, you simply had to close your eyes in bliss.

Chef Tham's culinary skills gave Second Grandmother the idea of persuading Sister Liu to become his apprentice. Sister Liu was intelligent and meticulous, and she had a rapport with Chef Tham, so before too long, Chef Tham began to develop feelings for her.

When our family's various daughters-in-law joined them in the kitchen, the two of them carried on as usual. When Grandfather's business expanded to Singapore in Nanyang, he brought Chef Tham with him. Grandfather's business in Nanyang didn't do as well as Grandfather had hoped, so Chef Tham went off to start a restaurant. Chef Tham's restaurant did well, you could say he was a self-made man. Not long after that, the rest of our family, led by both grandmothers, also came to Nanyang. Life was tough after the war. For us, the third generation born here in Nanyang, the memory of reunion dinners on Chinese New Year's Eve remains fresh in our minds. Chef Tham would prepare two pork trotters as a gift to our family, and each year it was Sister Liu who went to his restaurant to collect the dish. She took over the chef's task of serving the dish, flicking the meat off the bones. As we were small children back then, we had to wait for her to serve us, separating the meat from the bones. When she said one word: 'Good', we would raised our chopsticks, and say loudly: 'Thank you, Sister Liu'.

After Chef Tham's wife passed away, he came to ask Second Grandmother for permission to marry Sister Liu. Second Grandmother exclaimed to Sister Liu, 'The day you have long anticipated has finally come!' No one expected Sister Liu's answer to be no. She'd gotten used to being on her own, and the worst years were long gone, why should she make him happy now?

'My mistress may be the second wife, but that doesn't mean that I have to be one too,' Sister Liu said furiously to Auntie La. Auntie La said, 'If Chef Tham had made his offer ten years earlier, Sister Liu would have become his second wife.'

When Sister Liu died, Chef Tham sat on the edge of the huge water jar in our yard and bawled. His hair was white and looked as soft as if it had been woven out of flowers. His voice grew hoarse as he keened, 'My baby, my Frost Liu!' Sister Liu's name was Frost Liu. His heartache was extreme, and led Auntie La to say that his sort of misfortune was truly too much for anyone to bear.

FANS OF THE PHOENIX

IN THE SIXTIES AND SEVENTIES, our family's old address was across the road from Great World Amusement Park. From the second floor, you could see the park's enchanting lights. The ferris wheel made its rounds, the carousel horses made their rounds, and the ghost train went in and out of the dark woods. These were the dreamscapes of our childhood.

When we girl cousins get together, we like to chat about the old days when all of us lived together in that house. We go back over the big things and small things, our quarrels, our joys, our laughs, our smiles, and our tears. Maybe it's because of the problems we face in our present lives, maybe this is why we are nostalgic. Speaking of the past, we often bring up the subject of Ninth Uncle. Not because he was our mentor or anything serious like that. Simply because he taught us how to have fun.

He taught all the older cousins, starting from Cousin Xunru, how to dance. He said: 'The moment the band starts to play, your whole body must start to float. Don't think about anything else. Use your ears to listen to the beat, move your hands first, then the rest of your body, and lastly, your feet. You mustn't move your feet with force, because if you do that, you'll sound like a soldier on parade.'

We little ones would be sprawled out on the bed, watching Ninth Uncle teach the older cousins how to dance: 'One, two, three, turn, one, two, three, four, five, six, turn to the end.'

We were so taken with his commands that we copied him when

we scolded people: 'One, two, three, stupid egg, go to hell, one, two, three.'

Before going to a tea dance, the elder cousins would get Ninth Uncle to inspect their clothes – skirts, earrings, shoes. Cousin Biru walked before him in her cropped toga top in burnished gold and a billowing full black skirt with a houndstooth hemline in multiple colours, all seven shades of the rainbow, and gold stilettos four inches high.

Ninth Uncle pranced towards her, took her hand and made her twirl, turning her skirt into a mesmerising melody of colour. Next, Ninth Uncle reached out to remove one of her earrings, explaining: 'Wearing one earring is more attractive, it'll make people notice this shoulder.'

We do not have naturally good looks. But thanks to Ninth Uncle we learnt lots about looking good, which boosted our confidence, so that wherever we went, whether it was to tea dances or anywhere else, we already gave ourselves seventy points.

We often speak about Ninth Uncle to this day not because he was especially good to us, but because he was part of our childhood and youth, and he disappeared at a time when we were all so impressionable. We continue to miss those dreamlike days.

There are two possible reasons for his disappearance: first, he felt he owed our family too much, he would never be able to repay us, so he might as well run away from us. The other reason would be that there were just too many of us living together in that house. He couldn't stand it any longer, whether it was having to meet Grandfather's expectations of him, or to respond to us girl cousins' cries for attention, there was always someone who wanted a piece of him – 'Ninth Uncle!' 'Ninth Brother!' Maybe he couldn't take it, how intertwined our lives were.

We weren't the only ones who liked to talk about him. Auntie La also often reminisced about him. She was closer in age to him. They were confidantes. Sister Liu said that when they were little, they fought at one end of the bed and reconciled by the time they reached the other end. One minute they would be quarreling till their faces and ears turned red, next minute they would be hugging and laughing. That was just how they were.

Auntie La said she always gave in to him because she was older than him. She pinched him only when she was sure they were alone. He bruised easily – he had the kind of skin that turned black from a slight pinch. She had a gregarious and fiery personality, so whenever they played together, he would end up being her victim.

Whenever she told us stories about Ninth Uncle, Auntie La's face would turn serious and mysterious. With his powdery white pallor, Ninth Uncle reminded us of nineteenth-century vampires. He was flippant and proud at the same time, traits which we felt he'd inherited from his mother. No one else behaved like this in our family. Speaking of his mother, this was a woman who could have been accepted into our family where all her needs would have been taken care of. But she refused the offer when it was presented to her. We knew her as someone who could have been one of us but had said no. This added to our sense of Ninth Uncle as a mythical figure, somehow.

Ninth Uncle came to the big house when he was five. Before that he lived with his guardian, a Cantonese opera artiste who played the female roles. At age five, Ninth Uncle was already a fully-formed person with the traits that always made him stand out: he was aloof, arrogant, wilful, and if something merited his scorn and disdain, he didn't mask his feelings. Auntie La said that he looked at the world with cold eyes, and that no one could really tell what he was thinking. He was a voyeur who never got involved. She also said that he was lucky he came to live with us. Who else would have tolerated a child like that, one who was so narcissistic and proud?

Sister Liu said Ninth Uncle came to live with us after he fell very ill when he was five and had to undergo surgery in a hospital. After his blood type became known, the opera artiste realised Ninth Uncle wasn't his, so after Ninth Uncle recovered from his illness, he thought about it for a while, and then he contacted Grandfather and Second Grandmother because he simply couldn't get over the hurt and humiliation of having spent five years of his life raising a kid who wasn't his own. Grandfather and Second Grandmother immediately brought Ninth Uncle home. And Second Grandmother doted on the boy. She said yes to all his requests, she gave him everything he asked for. Sometimes she seemed to treat him better than the rest of the children in the family.

Sister Liu was Second Grandmother's maid and she liked to talk, so from her we learnt that the opera artiste was a petty person. Back when he and Grandfather were in a love triangle with Ninth Uncle's mother, he had claimed that he loved the woman selflessly, but look at how quickly he abandoned that woman's own flesh and blood when he learned the truth about Ninth Uncle. If Grandfather did a blood test and found out that he and Ninth Uncle weren't related, where else could Ninth Uncle go?

Since he was little, Ninth Uncle never had trouble with his studies. He was naturally bright and he had a photographic memory. He could easily master anything, good or bad, black or white. Second Grandmother enrolled him in a Roman Catholic mission school where he did well in all his subjects, especially languages. He brought cassette tapes of English and Japanese lessons home and made new ones of himself reciting the lessons. No one could tell which ones had been made by his teachers and which ones had been made by Ninth Uncle.

His first job was being a DJ at the English radio station where he was in charge of a song dedication programme. Second Grandmother said to him, 'As if it isn't bad enough that you've introduced so many soppy love songs to your audience, you've led so many girls astray, teaching them to sing those songs day in day out, don't you think you've caused enough trouble?' At that time, the songs he played frequently were 'Seven Lonely Days', and 'How Much Is That Doggy in the Window?'

His nickname was Prince of the Waves and he had scores of fans. Many young girls tuned in to his song dedication programme with stacks of books beside them. That was the era before television, when Ninth Uncle used his voice to captivate his listeners. I often saw my older cousins burrow under their blankets with a radio.

In our family the people who could sing were Auntie La, Ninth Uncle and my father, but my father loved to sing art songs and he always sang the tenor parts. Whenever his choir performed in public, my father would have the opportunity to lead the choir or sing a solo part. He was always the centre of attention. At of these concerts, he was given a solo part in 'The Whole River Red'. Every day at home he would belt out the famous lyrics and Ninth Uncle would cheekily harmonise with him. This pleased my father so much that he asked Ninth Uncle to join him on stage. Their item was meant to be in the middle of the programme, but it was moved to the penultimate time slot so when it was time for the two of them to perform, the atmosphere in the concert hall was electric and the audience cheered and clapped loudly. They provided the best possible warm-up for the choir's final song. According to Auntie La, there was a photo of my father and Ninth Uncle the next day in the papers – my father was of average height, Ninth Uncle was lanky; one of them was stocky, the other one had pretty features. Auntie La said that there were many copycat male duos who were formed after that, all of them inspired by my father and Ninth Uncle.

Earlier on it was mentioned that Second Grandmother complained about Ninth Uncle's singing. Later on, he would sing at home: 'Come back! I'm waiting for you!' All the girl cousins said, 'You've never seen him after he's just gotten out of bed, wearing his baggy pyjama bottoms rolled up to his knees, feet clad in slippers, standing at the window with bare shins, as pale as blanched chicken drumsticks, singing loudly, "Tell me how to forget him…"' It was the sort of art song that made everyone's skin crawl – far cringier than any pop song.

One time, the smaller cousins were hanging out at the balcony on the top floor. The sky was pink and then it turned purple, and

Ninth Uncle was at the door downstairs, walking on the street. His shiny black hair was combed stylishly. He wore a shirt with a green collar and his trousers were metallic bronze, and over his arm, he carried a brown jacket. In that warm golden dusk, he had his shades on and he turned and waved at us.

Ninth Uncle was a creature of the night. He knocked off at one or two in the morning. Sometimes we woke up in the middle of the night, feeling peckish, and if we were to go look for some biscuits to eat, we would smell his cologne along the corridor leading to the kitchen. There were times when we bumped into him in the kitchen and he would be there drinking, smoking, sometimes nibbling on a biscuit himself. In the night his face looked even paler, his lips even redder because of the wine. I never dared to watch zombie or vampire movies, and used to think that this probably had a lot to do with the impression he had given me back then.

He was really quite a character. Though he had his serious moments, most of the time he had an irrepressible sense of fun, and it was his nature not to take things seriously, to be flippant and playful. This was impossible to change!

Auntie La said he had so many girlfriends you could give them queue numbers. He wasn't serious about any of them. When girls came to look for him, he was never home, so Auntie La had to receive them and listen to their woes about him. She got sick and tired of listening to them, and she advised them to dump him. But she said the more you advised them to free themselves from him, the more they clung on. It was Second Grandmother who ordered Ninth Uncle to move out, because she had had enough of these visits from heartbroken girls.

Sister Liu had another theory about Ninth Uncle's departure.

She was sure he had run away because of his gambling debts. He left in the middle of the night when everyone in the Big House was fast asleep. He didn't take much with him, only his guitar, two or three suits, and a few pairs of shoes.

He wore size nine shoes. His feet were uncommonly large. He

left behind many pairs of shoes that were either new or hardly used. One of them was made of black and white patent leather. If you looked at them from the left, you saw only the white leather; from the right, they were black. One of the boy cousins, Zijian, kept that pair with him for the longest time, hoping that his feet would grow big enough for him to wear them. But no one in our family had feet as big as Ninth Uncle. No wonder he could walk such a long way away from us.

Sometimes we wished so hard that he would return, but as the years went by, and Second Grandmother and Sister Liu passed away, we resigned ourselves to reality. Why should he come back? Who was left for him to come back to see? Cousin Biru said that it might be better for us to remember him as a phoenix in our minds, better for us to forget his dark side, to remain forever bedazzled.

JADE AND FATE

1.

I WAS A SICKLY CHILD and lacked self-confidence, so my mother made me wear a jade pendant. She believed that the jade would protect me. I'm not sure why, but not long after I started wearing it, the jade became tarnished, its green turning dull like it had been contaminated by mould. My mother saw this as all the proof she needed to bolster her belief that wearing a piece of jade around my neck was something I should do, all the time, for the rest of my life. She bought new jade pendants for me, each one larger than the one before. Every day, it didn't matter what my outfit was, Mother's jade pendant would be hanging from my neck. With an unbuttoned shirt collar, it was even more conspicuous. It used to embarrass me, but after a while, I got used to it and hardly thought about taking it off anymore.

Most of all, I just wanted to be free of my mother's nagging, especially since my sister, who was ten years older than me, often chimed in. They ganged up on me, skinning me alive. My sister was from the same mould as my mother. She spoke at breakneck speed like my mother and she was just as high-strung. When both of them got together, sesame-small things turned into big problems. It was obvious that they enjoyed attacking me from all sides.

That day, it couldn't have been worst luck for Xijuan and me that my mother and sister were both at home when we went to my home. She became the object of their abuse:

'Never seen a girl with such a large mouth before,' my sister began.

'I agree, and her teeth are crooked. The front ones look like a book.'

'Her skin is okay, too bad her arms and legs are so hairy.'

'Really? I didn't notice. All I could think of was the size of her mouth. If she keeps quiet, maybe people won't notice how large it is.'

Before that I used to think that Xijuan's looks were average, and that she was kind and always ready to come and meet me whenever I asked her out. She had some coy mannerisms, which was also something I rather liked about her. I also liked her eyes, especially when she gave me one of those suggestive side glances. Sometimes she brushed her breasts against my body, seemingly by accident. Without going into too much unnecessary detail, there was, at such times, an expected effect of the physical kind. If I were candid, even the slightest touch of her shoulder could arouse me. It was tantalising to feel the nearness of her body – there it was just behind a layer of clothes. That feeling of being so close and yet so far made me crave for her even more. I was sure the feeling was mutual.

Anyway, that day when she came to my home, it was, as I said, to get my goggles, which I'd forgotten to put inside my bag when I went to meet her. I was the sort of person who had to do everything properly or not do them at all. Without my goggles I wouldn't have been able to swim. We were on our way to the pool near my place, so we went back for the goggles.

The moment we stepped through the door, I saw my mother and sister in the living room, busy folding paper ingots. They were probably planning to go to some temple again. Naturally, Mother's prayers would all be about me, whereas my sister would be praying for herself. She was keen to start a family and even keener on having just boys. They were thoroughly surprised to see Xijuan, but soon they recovered and began to scrutinise her from head to toe. Usually, Xijuan took care with her appearance whenever we met. I mean, she was the sort who wore stockings. But today we were going to the pool so she was casually dressed in a tee-shirt and shorts. She wasn't wearing any make-up. I could tell that Mother and my sister were unimpressed.

When I joined them in the living room after retrieving the goggles from my room, Xijuan was holding an ingot. I noticed for the first time how large her mouth was when she said, 'I often help my mother with these. She likes to go to Wang Da Xian, or else she would also consult the fortune-tellers at the temple. My father says it's absurd that she's prayed at all the temples in Hong Kong.'

At her words, my mother's face changed colour and my sister's brow creased into a frown. As I was trying my best to hurry Xijuan out of our flat, she was smiling and saying to my mother and sister, 'I'll come again another time.'

There was no reply from either of them. I was practically pushing Xijuan out of the flat and she was still talking about how alike our families were. She said the only difference was that she had a father. I wished she'd been less warm and friendly as my mother and sister would be less hurtful if she had been cold and aloof. That was just how they were.

Once we got to the pool and jumped into the water, I forgot all my unhappiness. When Xijuan came out of the changing room, she was in a red swimsuit and I was bowled over by how good she looked: her porcelain skin against the red of her swimsuit, the blue water, all combined to give me a feeling of inexpressible exhilaration. I made her hold on to me as I moved towards the deeper end. As she couldn't swim, she hugged me tightly. With her arms around my neck and her soft breasts pressing into my back, the touch of skin on skin, the envious looks of the other men in the pool, and the reaction of our bodies to one another... All of this made me think: as long as she didn't speak too much or went around trying to please everyone, she was a good catch.

After the swim I brought her to a steakhouse. When I got home my mother and sister pounced on me.

'Are you going to marry this girl?' my mother asked.

'Mother, we're just friends.'

'She seemed to be very sure of herself. The way she behaved in our home was so presumptuous.'

'Mother! What's wrong with you? We just came back here to get my goggles.'

'You have terrible taste in women. Your last girlfriend was small and dark, now this one has such a huge face and mouth.'

'I'm not going to say anything more. Nothing that I do is good enough for you.'

I was used to it. Since I was young my mother had never praised me. She was the same way with my father when he was alive.

My father worked as a postman. He often said being a postman was very meaningful as he was entrusted with bringing people together through their letters, and he performed this role no matter how great the distance. It is for this reason that I'd regarded my father as a great man since I was a boy. In kindergarten, we sang a nursery song about postmen, and my classmates were envious that I had a postman as my father. I was very smug about it too, until one day, my mother, father, and I were at the public housing board in order to make an appeal for a larger flat. I was already in secondary school, it wasn't appropriate for us to share a bedroom with our parents.

We had made an application for a larger flat which hadn't been approved. It was that rejection letter that my mother clutched in her hands. And I could see the rejection letter shaking when her hands began to shake, after the officer treated us as if we were beggars on a street corner and told us there was nothing he could do for our case. My mother's hands shook not because she was afraid of that man, but because she was furious. When she opened her mouth to speak, she looked like a lioness.

'My husband is a postman. He has slaved his whole life for the good of everyone, including you. And now you are saying that you can't help us. But I can see that you are all very anxious to help the boat people! You must think we're so stupid!'

After that she turned on my father.

'You're so stupid! Stupid, stupid man! Spent your whole life being a postman? Much better to be a refugee! Just get in line and wait to be fed and housed for free. We're the stupidest ones! They say they care about the common people, but look at us now! We've been paying our taxes, paying them to who? It's all a scam. Listen to you talk, like you know anything! You think a postman is somebody, do you? Let me tell you, they're telling you to piss off!'

Everyone was staring at my parents but my mother didn't stop screaming her head off. Eventually the three of us were invited into a room.

A year later, our appeal was approved and we were allocated a flat that was twice the size of our old one. The story of how we managed to succeed in our appeal was told by Mother to all our neighbours. She claimed all the credit, of course. This was my mother being my mother. All her life she had gotten her way by behaving like a tyrant. Whilst I was still schooling, she watched over me like a hawk. She knew all my teachers and made sure she stayed in contact with them on a regular basis. Once, when I was in Sec One, I was allocated a seat at the back of the classroom. After my mother learnt about it, she told the teacher that I was cock-eyed and shouldn't be seated so far away from the blackboard. There was nothing wrong with my eyes; everyone knew she was lying. Still, my teacher moved me in the end. It was understandable. My mother kept calling my teacher and pestering him. And all because she was worried I wouldn't pay attention if I was seated at the back. No thanks to her, I was teased by my classmates for being a mummy's boy. She came to eat lunch with me every day. When I begged her not to come, she actually confronted my classmates and gave their names to the teacher.

After my father died, she had less time. She went out to work, and for once in my life I was free. But not long after that my sister learnt all her tricks and my life in school became a nightmare all over again. She eavesdropped on my phone conversations, which was how she found out that I had decided to major in the Humanities like most of my friends. History and Literature were the subjects I enjoyed the most and I knew that I would do well if I pursued my interests. But my sister told my mother about my decision. She flew into a rage.

'Do you want to end up being a worthless postman like your father? Your results are good enough for you to go into the Science stream and yet you want to choose the Humanities. What's wrong with you?'

I knew that I would do badly at the final exams before the results were released. The classmates who did worse than me in the past all managed to get their university places because they had gone into the Humanities stream. I would have been fine if not for my mother and sister's interference. When I got home, I shouted at them before they could react to my grades.

'Don't you dare tell me off! If it weren't for you, I wouldn't have gone into the Sciences and none of this would have happened! It's all your fault! If you say anything more, I'm going to jump off this building!'

I slammed the door on my way out.

I didn't come home till it was one in the morning. For the first time in her life my mother spoke to me softly: 'I'm not mad at you because I know you tried your best. Would you like a bowl of chicken and chestnut soup? It's your favourite. I've been slow cooking it for four hours.'

How could I refuse my mother, the one who had raised me to never say no to her? Of course I drank the soup.

2.

I was well suited for my job. As a librarian, I had to be familiar with computers as all the libraries had been modernised. Because I was a Science student, I didn't find it hard to work with computers, unlike my colleagues who had studied the Humanities. Besides, my mother had paid for computer lessons. My colleagues came to me whenever they had questions about computers. I began to feel like I was someone whom people looked up to. It gave me a sense of satisfaction.

At home I was a different person too. I told my mother during dinner time about how I had been consulted by my colleagues whenever they ran into difficulties with the computer system. My mother was quick to claim credit, which was hardly surprising.

'Hah, I knew that those computer lessons would come in handy.'

I didn't argue with her. Apart from those computer lessons, I also became adept at using the computer because I familiarised myself with its functions. Why should I tell her this? It was more filial to let her be. Of course, I never considered how it was probably because my father had indulged her that my mother became so overbearing.

We had a new colleague, someone who would guide us in the transition to the fully digital catalogue system. She had received her training in England. Her name was Carefree Yu.

We were all surprised to learn that she was our supervisor the first time we met her. Her hair was very short. And she wasn't like the other supervisors. She didn't bother learning our names. All she cared about was the computing system. On her first day at the library, she went through her work plan and said that we were to commence work on it right away.

She didn't care if anyone was fearful of computers. She would say, 'What's the big deal? If you key in a mistake, just delete it and do it again. The important thing is to learn from your mistakes and move on.'

She wanted us to switch completely to computers within a fortnight. She didn't think it was too soon: 'The learning curve is always steepest at the start. After one month, you'll all be wondering how you ever got any work done without computers!'

She was right. For those of us who were used to working with computers, it would feel very strange if we were told to not use them anymore.

Carefree was also different from most people in that her self-confidence and ruthlessness were of a package with her forthright manner. What I had noticed since I started working was that people either had a lot of self-confidence and lacked ruthlessness, or they were ruthless and lacked ability and substance. Whenever Carefree spoke, she would keep her gaze steady and focused so that you felt you couldn't say no to her, nor could you say anything that wasn't the truth. As long as you were willing to perform the task she assigned to you, she would be patient with you, give you advice and allow you to have time to get the job done.

That was how she was with Alice, the colleague who was most computer-resistant. Every lunchtime, Alice would complain about Carefree. Soon, Carefree must have gotten wind of this. She arranged for Alice to spend an hour each day with her, and she personally coached Alice. A month later, Alice was totally converted. In the past, Alice would spend the last half hour of each work day going to the toilet to comb her hair and powder her face or washing her mug at the pantry. After that one month of personal computer tuition with Carefree, Alice would still be glued to her screen when it was time to knock off. Even if the other colleagues told her it was time to go home, she would be reluctant to leave. Ah, human beings! Human beings are capable of change. Of course, it would be too much to expect Alice to turn into a fan. No, it was already quite something that she no longer bitched about her.

Carefree never made lunch appointments. She would ask around close to lunchtime to see if anyone was free. She looked perfectly comfortable on the days when she ate lunch on her own, reading the newspaper after she finished her food, drinking coffee. One day, I was free and we went out for lunch together. After our orders were placed, her gaze fell on my neck and she said, 'That's so ugly! Why don't you get rid of it?'

At first I was shocked into silence. What she said was something that had never crossed my mind all these years. No one had ever spoken to me like that before. Throw the jade away, just like that. I didn't know what I was supposed to say. I looked at the jade pendant.

'Is it really so ugly?' I asked.

'Is it meant to ward off evil?' she asked with a smirk, sipping her coffee.

'My mother made me wear it because I was often sick when I was a child.'

'What about now? Do you fall sick easily?'

'These days? I've not had flu in two years. Are you saying I should stop wearing the jade?'

'I just think it's quite an eyesore. Whether you should carry on wearing it is something you have to decide for yourself, isn't it? You are free to choose, surely, if you want to look like a character from *Dream of Red Chambers* or a modern man in the twentieth century. Guys don't really wear jewellery these days.'

'Don't you like Jia Baoyu?'

'I prefer Mount Tai,' she said, bursting into laughter.

At home I looked at my body in the mirror. Without the jade pendant, I looked good. It was the first time I realised this. I looked clean and healthy, at least to myself. I had a tan from swimming all summer. But there were two blemishes: the thin pale line where the necklace obstructed the sun, and also where the jade rested.

I liked what I saw – I had a nice-looking body, and without the jade pendant, I looked even better. But I also couldn't help wondering if I felt this way because it was truly what I wanted or if this new way of thinking was due to what she had said. I didn't want to stop wearing the jade just because of her remarks.

I put the jade back on and got dressed. Then I heard Mother

knocking at my bedroom door.

'Hey, what are you doing inside? Didn't you hear me calling you to come and drink the soup? Are you asleep?'

'What soup?'

'I made a special soup for you. Chicken and hasma. I see how hard you've been working and I thought I'd make you this tonic soup.'

'Mother, don't make such expensive soups in future. A simple cooling soup with carrot and radish would be fine.'

'Those soups are too cooling for you. Your body is weak.'

'Who says so? I've not been sick in years.'

'Shh! What are you saying? Asking for trouble!'

'Mother, is it okay for me to stop wearing this jade?'

'No! Don't you dare take it off!'

'One day I will.'

'You'd better not do that. If not for the jade's protection, how do you think you grew to be so tall?'

'Why don't you say I grew tall because of your soups?'

'Don't you dare take it off! Who taught you this nonsense?'

'Mother, it's really very ugly. Look, don't you think it's ugly? I went into a boutique the other day to try on a silk shirt. The salesgirl kept saying how the pendant clashed with the shirt. My colleague also teased me. She said it was very odd for a grown man to be wearing a large piece of jade.'

'What do they know? Why don't you ask Xijuan? Does she mind that you wear jade? Enough of this nonsense, come, let's have dinner.'

Speaking of Xijuan, there was certainly a change in my mother and sister's attitude towards her. She came to our place frequently, and sometimes she brought her mother's homecooked braised duck and yam dessert, which made Mother and my sister look forward to her visits. They love Teochew food, and Xijuan's mother was Teochew.

As for me, I didn't feel like I wanted things to progress between us. I didn't know why. Sometimes when my mother wasn't at home, Xijuan and I would be alone in my bedroom. Whilst I was teaching her how to use the computer, she would suddenly kiss me. I kissed her back and caressed her body, but that was all I felt like doing. Something held me back, I wasn't sure what it was, but it was a strong force and I didn't go against it. One time, Xijuan unbuttoned her blouse and I almost gave in, but then I raised my head and saw the computer, and immediately my desire for her flagged into nothing. I lifted her and did up her buttons.

She went home crying that night. I had to making comforting sounds as she kept saying it was her fault. She asked, 'Do you think badly of me because I'm being so forward? Do you despise me? Do you see me as a slut? Will you still see me after tonight? Are you going to steer clear of me in future?'

'Go home, and don't think too much, everything is okay.'

At her doorstep she dried her tears and blurted, 'I know what this is. You don't love me!'

I wanted to say no, but she went in and I was left outside, facing her door.

Xijuan, computers, the jade pendant, Carefree. These things kept going round and round in my head. I was so troubled, I had to remove the jade from my neck. More and more I was going to bed without the jade. I slept well. I could sleep on my side or on my chest, unlike before. The necklace used to give me the sensation of being strangled, or sometimes if I turned too suddenly, the jade would knock against my chest and wake me up. Sometimes the necklace got into a tangle with the jade and I would have to spend quite a lot of time and energy to separate them. I began to see that jade as a hassle to wear. Sometimes when I wore a white shirt, my reflection in the mirror would cause me to frown because all I could see was how ugly the jade was, and how it ruined my appearance.

And yet I continued to wear it, I didn't get rid of it!

3.

Carefree had been with our company for four months when she said she was leaving. When we asked her where she was going, she said she was going to Singapore. An international computing corporation had offered her a position there. We asked her if she was migrating to Singapore, she said she was going there just to work. Her horizons were limitless.

Speaking of migrating to Singapore, a few months ago, on the second day the forms were issued by their government, Mother went to queue for them on my behalf. The queue stretched from Admiralty Centre to Wanchai. Under the hot summer sun, she queued under an umbrella. When she got home, her entire face was flushed. I was furious.

'I told you not to get these forms. Why wouldn't you listen to me? There were so many people there, and you had to queue for several hours. How could you take it?'

'I was worried for you, how would you have been able to find the time to go and queue? Anyway I have nothing to do at home, so I went and got them for you. Now you must fill them up as soon as possible and quickly submit them. Let me fix something for you to eat.'

That night Mother had a headache and fever. I was very upset. I went through the forms: the blue ones were a set of eight pages, the yellow ones had six pages. From our family annals, I found our old address. I had to find my birth certificate, identity papers, passport, educational certificates, and fill in my work experience. There were photocopies to be made. It took me a whole week to get everything in order for submission. At the reception desk, I asked the woman who stamped my thick folder of forms and supporting documents when I would hear back from them. She said the wait would be three months!

It really took three months. On the same day Carefree

announced she was leaving, I suddenly received a call from the Singapore emigration agency: 'We are sorry to inform you that your application has been rejected. Please come to our office to collect your refund of $1,200 and your documents.'

Two pieces of unhappy news on the same day. I couldn't say which one affected me more. Both made me feel dejected.

Mother was especially disappointed. These few years she had pinned her hopes all on me. But I seemed to be doing worse than my father. His job as a postman was the reason we could move to a bigger apartment. With my $7,000 monthly salary, my qualifications and five years' work experience, I couldn't meet the requirements to migrate to Singapore.

The woman at the agency said: 'You have to find a job in Singapore first. When you have $1,500 in Singapore dollars, you can apply again. Then you will stand a better chance of being approved.'

I felt low. To be rejected was very upsetting. Carefree consoled me: 'Perhaps when I'm there, I can find you a job. What you lack are professional qualifications. Since you're so interested in computers, you should get a professional certificate in computing. You've been working for a few years now, you should have some savings.'

For a twenty-three-year-old, going back to school shouldn't be too late. Furthermore, I was sure my mother had savings. There was money from my father's insurance payout. If I asked her to fund my studies in Canada or America, I was sure she would say yes. She thought I had given up on further studies after my poor results. Actually, I was fine. When she heard that I wished to go to university she was elated, as expected.

'Go to Canada. Auntie Cheng and Auntie Fang are both in Canada, they will help you find a good university over there. Canada, good choice!'

'Mother, just look at you. Can you please stop meddling, I'll handle my own application.'

'The money from your father's insurance policy, you can use it.'

'Mother, I'm worried about you.'

'Your sister will look after me. I forgot to tell you, she's expecting. After she gives birth, I'll look after her baby, she'll be going back to work. You don't have to worry about me.'

There is always a way. In life, one must take one step at a time. Things will always work out in the end. I suddenly felt released. Unknowingly, a change had taken place. I felt more grounded somehow.

Carefree was leaving. We organised a farewell party for her. It was the end of September, but it was still very hot. Alice suggested renting a yacht and everyone cheered.

These few months I saw her at work every day. We got along very well, and on some days we went for drinks together. She liked to have beer after work, she told me.

'I like the sensation of the first sip of an ice-cold beer, going straight into my body. It's very good, very satisfying.'

After one or two cigarettes – she liked al fresco bars – she would say, 'Let the night cover you gently. There's a feeling of being surrounded by nature.'

I liked her too much. Or perhaps I should say, I was in love with her. But I couldn't bring myself to say it, I knew I wouldn't be able to hold on to her. I wasn't nature, and I definitely wasn't Mount Tai. She told me, 'This is a first for me, being friends with someone as young as you. My friends are all older than me, and far more successful and mature than me. I've learnt a lot from them.'

Undeniably, hanging out with older people was a good way to learn new things; this had been my experience with her. Usually after work, we would go for drinks, chat for a while and then head home separately. Once I got home, I looked forward to seeing her again the next day.

And to think, she would leave me so very soon!

The yacht for her farewell had been rented by Alice. It cost $3,000, not bad for a boat with onboard shower facilities. The yacht stopped near a small island, the name of which was unknown to us, and everyone swam towards its beach. Carefree was a good swimmer, she loved the sea. Everyone was swimming towards the shore, whilst she kept insisting on heading towards a cliff on the other side. No one else followed her, only me. She was clearly someone who sailed a lot. She found her way carefully around the craggy rocks and after she climbed onto the largest one, she called out to the rest of our colleagues like a child. But no one swam over. They seemed happy with the spot they had chosen.

Because I wasn't tired, I carried on swimming in the sea. Recently I had learnt the butterfly stroke and I wished to perform it in this broad expanse of sea. I moved my hips vigorously and flung my arms forwards. I was like a dolphin moving forwards, propelling myself with my rear movements. I felt very happy. I even wished that I could strip off my trunks, because they encumbered me and my member which seemed to desire to be part of the sport outside.

In the sea that day, it was the first time I felt that my will and my actions were united. In that instant, I liked myself a lot.

I realised she was gazing at me from her position on that large rock. I swam towards her, carefully clambering onto that rock. I was happy, truly. My whole body was dripping with seawater and I was standing face-to-face with her. 'Ha, really happy,' I said.

'You know what? You really looked like dolphin earlier on!'

'A what?'

'A dolphin! You looked like something strong and intelligent.'

'Really? Ah!' I laughed and looked straight back at her.

I bent my head as I brushed the pearls of water on my body. I spied my jade. I took it off, held it in my hand, thinking that now would be the perfect moment to throw it into the sea.

'Thinking of chucking it?'

'Yes. Ever since that first time you mentioned it, I've been thinking that one day I must definitely get rid of it.'

'Why haven't you thrown it away all this time?'

'I was afraid my mother would scold me.'

'What about now? How are you going to explain to her?'

'I've been hinting to her that one day I'll get rid of this piece of jade. I mustn't break her heart.'

'Is that so?' Her fingers moved across my neck, over the places in contact with the jade and the necklace. I kissed them lightly.

She said, 'Jade means desire!'

'What do you mean?' I was stunned.

'Jade means desire. Their Chinese characters are homophones.'

I had a sudden flash of understanding. Mother's desires, my desires, they were fused inside this piece of jade. This gave me pause.

'Do you still want to throw it away? This jade,' she took the jade from me and kissed it. Her gesture made my heart go wild, and I thought then that if she gave me permission, I would love her for eternity. But then I also suddenly recalled that her name was Carefree Yu and I was overcome by sadness. She seemed to be aware of how I was feeling: 'You can't bear to lose this piece of jade?'

'No. I am attached to its significance.'

'Keep it then. Even if you don't destroy it, it's fine. How many people can be as cavalier as Jia Baoyu?'

There and then I just felt that I needed her very badly, spiritually and sexually.

I looked towards the shore. Because of the rising tide, our throng of colleagues on the beach seemed to be more distant from us than before. The craggy rocks provided a space of concealment for us. Carefree was wearing a black bikini. Her skin was tanned from the summer sun.

I rested my chin on her shoulder. There were tan-lines which gave her skin two different tones. A thin white line separated her shoulders, and the bronzed skin beyond it sandwiched the line like delectable chocolate separated by a layer of butter. I couldn't hold back anymore, I began to kiss her all over. In that instant, I fulfilled her vision of me, as an intelligent and energetic dolphin.

Whilst I lay down to rest, looking at the blue sky, Carefree Yun sat beside me, staring at the sea. I caressed her back tenderly, I felt exuberant. I had given my first time to her. Naturally it wasn't her first time, but I was so willing to let her have mine, she was worth it. I remembered then that I hadn't felt the same way about Xijuan; that was so that I could preserve myself for Carefree Yu. But the fact that we got together at this time, in this place, in this moment, hadn't been planned. My eyes suddenly fell upon that piece of jade on the rock, surrounded by the beating waves.

The tide rose higher, inch by inch the sea grew higher and closer to the rock surface. We slipped back into the water, swam to the shore, joined the throng of people there, and spent the rest of that afternoon as if nothing had happened. Yet in my heart, I felt at ease. I was contented, and from time to time I looked over at Carefree Yu.

There had been a breakthrough for both my mind and my body, I felt sure of it. I had matured. Over this one day, I gained immeasurable confidence in myself.

On our way back, I asked Carefree Yu to follow me to the stern. The sky was a pale lilac hue. I held the jade in my hand. I said to her: 'Come, watch me as I throw it into the sea, returning it to nature.'

I forcefully flung the jade pendant away, and turned back to look at Carefree Yu. Two crystalline tears rolled from her eyes. She wiped them away and smiled at me. We were about to say something to each other, but Alice came looking for us, yelling: 'Hey! Time for the group photo.' We were snapped as the sun set.

That night I sent Carefree Yu home. As we were both fatigued, I didn't stay for long. On the walls in her home I saw this scroll: 'What seems false can be real; what seems real can be false. What one owns can be an illusion; an illusion can turn out to be one's true possession.'

Did these words sum up Carefree Yu's life philosophy? I would need more time and effort before I could understand their meaning. I already knew very clearly that it wouldn't be impossible to make her mine. Ever since I threw away that piece of jade, I seemed to have a clearer understanding of the complexity of relationships, the ways that lives could be irrevocably entangled. To be honest, should Carefree Yu disappear from my life the next day, I would still feel grounded inside my heart.

On my way home, the sound of the nightly news wafted through from TV sets behind store windows, reporting that tomorrow the British would announce how many Hong Kongers would receive the permit to be UK residents. I had no part in that, I belonged to Hong Kong. I was born here, and that craggy rock where I became a grown man, that piece of jade which I had flung away, they were on this island, in this country, in the sea here. My feelings could be summed up by the verses of Zhang Xiaoxiang: 'By now I was used to the hardship of life; and yet I found consolation from the beauty of mountains and lakes.'

My mother was upset about that piece of jade for a long time. Then again, she was overwhelmed, not long afterwards, by a different source of joy, for my sister gave birth to a boy, and Mother could pin her hopes on the baby. The most curious thing: at the baby's first month celebration, Mother drew a piece of jade out of her handbag, and very carefully, she tied it around that tiny neck. Mother and my sister beamed with heartfelt satisfaction. Jade!

CLOVE

IF I WERE TO SEE HER AGAIN, I must make her stay!

It was dusk that day when she accompanied me to the street to hail a taxi. Singapore's Orchard Road is truly a pretty street. A boulevard of shopping malls and hotels with trees, with the lilac skies of dusk up above, it was a lovely scene just before nightfall, when the lights had yet to come on. After I got inside the taxi, she didn't leave but stood on the kerb and watched. The traffic light was red then, and the taxi didn't move. It was then that I noticed her goose yellow dress, a green belt tied loosely at her waist. She waved.

Her name is Yu Dingxiang, her father is Yu Wenjue, a world-class jewellery designer. Ten years ago, our family ran a jewellery business in Hong Kong, but the business folded due to my father's gambling debts and all the staff were scattered, and Yu Wenjue was hired by Ruixing Gold Shop in Singapore; what about my father then? He was his usual easygoing self, going out every morning for breakfast with his birds, playing mahjong after lunch, boasting about his past glory days.

As for me, I was given his trademark for the business, and I started from scratch, but with a different focus. My brand name was 'De Bao Zhai' and I would focus on costume jewellery. I knew I needed outstanding designers to create beautiful and well-crafted pieces to attract customers, so I decided to look up Yu Wenjue in Singapore. Perhaps I should have seen it coming. He had worked all his life with gold and precious stones. Why should he switch to costume jewellery?

When he turned me down, I wasn't dejected, but I did sit in his living room in a daze.

Minutes passed, and it was he who began to feel sad on my behalf. As we talked, he took out some drawings to show me. I could feel myself waking up.

The sketches showed the influence of historical jewellery designs from different dynasties in China. They didn't look like his usual work. Yu said: 'These were drawn by Yu Dingxiang. She was just having some fun. She's an avid reader of books about classical Chinese jewellery. She came up with these designs by herself. What do you think of them?'

'They are fantastic, where is she? I must see her!'

Two long hours went by before she appeared and greeted me: 'Hello, Tang Shunzu.' I told her how much I loved her designs, she looked at me, her eyes were smiling, and she began to speak at length about her ideas:

'The colours from Dunhuang are the brightest.'

'The carving of flowers is a craft that will surely be back in fashion again, patterns can be copies of past designs!'

'The hairpin can be modified and made into necklaces and bracelets.'

'There needs to be a breakthrough with the floral designs in cloisonne. Look at this design: there are lotus flowers on the gold, and then there are colours like red, purple, blue, which provide contrast. For cloisonne, the colours must be painted on very quickly and with great skill.'

'This is a hair accessory worn by the Northern Zhou noble women. I found it in the annals of that time. Do you think it'll look good as a choker?'

'There are from the Tang dynasty. They're said to be the earrings of Ah Man, the famous Tang court dancer. I think we could just make imitations of this design, do you agree?'

As I listened to her, I felt sad all of a sudden. What had I been doing all those past years without the guidance of her brilliance?

I said to Yu Dingxiang: 'I want all your designs, I'll sign an agreement with you. In Hong Kong, I have some very competent artisans, they will certainly be able to produce worthy pieces with your drawings. I will not cut corners, I understand what is art. I don't have a lot of capital, but I have enough to turn your designs into costume jewellery. I have buyers in Japan and Europe who are always asking for products from me. In this day and age, all women like to wear ornaments. How many people can afford branded jewellery? Apart from royals and shipping magnates, people from that strata of society, I mean. And even in the latter category, there are some who wear fake gems.

'Our jewellery must have a strong oriental flavour. Our marketing will be similar to that of our western European competitors, except that we'll be telling them the story of jewellery in Asia. It's like what you told me: "In AD439, during the Northern Zhou dynasty, there was a nobleman with the surname Yuwen. His favourite concubine liked to wear this ornament on her head because it flattered her face shape. She credited it with making her popular with the emperor." Next year in Florence there will be a costume jewellery expo, I plan to take part with pieces made from your designs.'

Later on, she saw me off, and all I could think of was how I would always remember her. Ten years ago she was just a child, but now she was a young woman, and even if she were to paint her face, I would recognise her. Even if she were to be standing in a dark corner, I wouldn't miss her, I'm sure of it!

After our conversation, she walked with me out to the street, waited for me to hail a taxi, I couldn't describe how she looked, ten years ago I hadn't noticed her, besides back then she was very young, and the meeting so many years later also took place in haste, which meant I didn't have a chance to study her looks carefully; and yet, if I were to run into her elsewhere, even if she were wearing make-up, even if our meeting took place somewhere dimly-lit, I would recognise her for sure, I am very certain I would!

* * *

I brought her designs back to Hong Kong and showed them to my craftsmen. Old Uncle Yu cried when he saw them: 'What's wrong with our people today? Why do we copy the west mindlessly? Why don't we study our own national treasures? We're really useless, so very useless!'

And then: 'Yu's daughter drew these? Ah, the Yus, the Yus, their blood is thicker than ours! The heavens have not given up on De Bao Zhai. Even if I were to go blind, I will make sure these designs are turned into wonderful products.'

The first designs were launched with an advertising campaign on TV and the result was that they became highly sought after. The newspapers also interviewed me. There were questions which I knew how to answer but chose not to answer. The reporters asked:

'Your designs are easy to copy. How will you handle your rivals' copying your designs?' I smiled and refused to answer. There was no need for me to say anything. People who knew how to appreciate our products would be able to tell the difference.

'Your prices are very high for costume jewellery. Will you lower them in future?' On the contrary, I would raise our prices.

'We heard that your designer is in Singapore. How do the designs reach you in Hong Kong? Are they escorted by security officers?' Yu Dingxiang sent me her designs by post. Sometimes she drew on embossed serviettes from cafes.

'Where did your designer study? He seems to be well-versesd in Chinese history as well as antique jewellery; how old is he, I'm guessing he's around fifty?' Who would have guessed, she was a high school graduate, twenty-five this year.

After the seventy-second design, no more arrived. I became extremely agitated. My father noticed the change in me. He threw side glances at me, he never said a word and he would walk away. My heart was filled with hatred, for him, for De Bao Zhai, for myself. I was deeply unhappy.

I wrote several letters to her. Eventually a reply arrived from her. It contained only four Chinese characters in her handwriting: 'I am spent.'

I showed her letter to my father who was practising calligraphy in his study. He threw his head back and laughed and went on to write four Chinese characters with his ink brush: 'Know when to stop.'

It was only then that I felt guilt-stricken. What did I take her for? I deserved to die!

Father fetched books for me from his bookcase – plays, books about language and ideas, myths and legends et cetera. I opened a book about etymology of Chinese characters, my curiosity piqued.

Father said: 'In these volumes and plays, there are details about how women dressed. I suspect Dingxiang's illustrations were based on her reading of such books.'

'And this book of etymology is also significant. Don't underestimate it, you can look up the origins and evolution of the Chinese characters for gold, silver, pearl and jade, you will learn a lot.'

I looked up the character for the circular jade artefact, '璧 (*bi*)', popular in the Shang, Zhou and Han dynasties, originating in the Neolithic period. I recalled one of her drawings of a collar piece with a pendant at the centre. The sides were broad, the holes were small, and there were circles going through the holes, the marks were made of cloisonne blue, the colours of Dunhuang, round and big, worn around the neck, the piece would go well with a low-neck black top, it was gorgeous and wild.

Next I looked up the character '玦 (*jue*)', also a circular jade disc but with a gap on one side. I remembered that Dingxiang had a drawing which perplexed Old Uncle Yu. He studied her drawing for a period of time before he came up with a series of ornaments, bracelets and necklaces. They were special because they all had a missing element, it was what made them stand out.

I returned to my bedroom, and in the dark I murmured to her, calling for her, Yu Dingxiang.

Compared to my father, compared to Yu Wenjue, and most of all compared to Yu Dingxiang, I was the biggest idiot in the whole world.

It was only then that I realised why Yu Wenjue, Old Uncle Yu, and especially Yu Dingxiang, were so nice to me. They did it for Father's sake. As for me, ah! Whatever success I had achieved was all due to Father. He may have gambled away his business, but the name and standing of the shop remained untarnished. When I was young, I didn't fully appreciate Father's career; I dismissed his work as being coarse, and so I chose to read English in England. After his failure, I didn't show him any concern, whereas he kept his company's trademark for me, refusing to sell it to anyone. And he had done all this quietly, just so that I would be able to benefit from the stature of his brand.

The next day, I went to look for Old Uncle Yu and I asked him about what Father did when his business failed and I was still in England. Old Uncle Yu said:

'Yu Wenjue worked for your family for the longest time. You also know that he was like a brother to your father. He took care of design, your father took care of sales. Their collaboration allowed De Bao Zhai to become an established brand.

'After your father lost the business, the most furious person was Yu Wenjue. Your father kept apologising to him but he ignored your father.

'It's understandable, since Yu Wenjue did everything he could to build up De Bao Zhai, and in a moment of folly, your father destroyed it all. Let me tell you, people ah! You can take a wrong step, just one misstep, and everything is over.

'When Yu Wenjue left Hong Kong, he didn't tell anyone he was leaving. From this alone, you can tell how mad he was.'

I wrote to Dingxiang every day after that. I told her my news, no matter how mundane, and I told her what I learnt about her drawings from my study of my father's books.

When she finally replied, I felt a heavy burden was lifted from me!

As I left for Florence with a batch of exquisite pieces, I could only think of Yu Dingxiang. I had sent my people two months ago to Italy to take care of the publicity, and orders were already coming in. Everything was going the way I had hoped for, and I had also sent her an air ticket, for her to fly from Singapore, and for us to meet in Florence, which I had told her was the birthplace and hometown of Dante.

Yu Dingxiang asked me to recite a passage from Dante's *Divine Comedy* to her when we were in Florence. She knew I was an English graduate from Hong Kong University. I memorised a passage, not in English but in Italian, this would be a surprise to her, and I made sure that I could recite it even in my dreams; how difficult could that be? Back when I was a student, I had won a grant from the Italian government to do research on Dante in Florence.

Now, it was my time to repay my debt to her. Ah! My most beloved Yu Dingxiang, if I were to see her again, I must make her stay!

BATIK MELODY

1.

I STOOD BY THE SIDE, watching my stepmother Aisha as she cleaned Father's body. Next, the elders wrapped his body with a blue cotton cloth and turned his face towards Mecca.

Father looked serene. The white kufi on his head looked like it had been placed there with care. The white made his black eyebrows look even darker, even straighter. He looked like he had passed away peacefully.

I had come home two weeks before Father died. When I saw him, he could still speak, although his body was too weak for him to sit up. He said to me, 'You must manage this batik factory properly. The quality of our batik must be maintained. It must have character, there must always be something special about our batik. Apart from strong patterns, the effect of the dyes must also be good. Handmade batik is truly an art, the kind of batik made by machines cannot compare. You must understand this! When you have settled your things over there in the UK, I want you to move into this big house. I want you to take care of Aisha. These ten years she has helped me a lot. Without her, our business wouldn't have grown so big. And then there are your two half-sisters, Shalinah and Hayati. Although you are not related by blood, during the time you were away, they gave me a lot of joy and comfort. I want you to treat them well.

'There's something else that's very important to me. After my soul has returned to Mecca, I want you to go and open my cupboards. You will see all the materials I have been collecting all these years. I've been meaning to write a book about the history of batik in Nanyang. But now I am dying. My only hope is that you will write the book in my place. But remember, according to my research, the batik in Nanyang originates from Yunnan and Guizhou in China. You must trust me on this point. Last year your two sisters went to Yunnan with me and they agreed with my theory. You must believe me. Trust me! Otherwise I will not be able to go in peace.'

Over the next few days, his speech became incoherent. I stayed by his side, feeding him porridge and water. Because we were mentally prepared for the inevitable, when Father died, we didn't feel too shocked or sorrowful.

At this moment we were waiting for the casket to arrive. We were also waiting for our relatives. Father liked to be clean, so it would be best to hold his burial before the end of the day.

I observed my stepmother. She wore a black tudung, her head was bowed, but I could still see her long eyelashes and her pale face. She was said to be of Arabic descent, from the line of Juwairiah, one of Prophet Mohammed's wives. She lay her hands on her lap, they were clasped. There was calm in that gesture. She was only forty, and she had already had two husbands. Both marriages lasted ten years. Her elder daughter, Shalinah, was twenty and the younger one, Hayati, was eighteen; both of them were from her first marriage. I was my father's only child, his only son.

I turned my attention to my half-sisters.

Shalinah wore her glossy hair up in a bun. It was held in place by a leaf-shaped tortoiseshell clip. She was twenty-four but she dressed as if she was forty. Her ears were delicate, her eye lashes were very long. Whenever she raised her eyes to look at you, seemingly on impulse, there was a querulous air in her gaze.

Hayati tied her hair into two thick plaits. Like her sister, she didn't have bangs. Her face was young and clean, her brows were very arched and thick, her nose had a high bridge. From all angles her mouth wore a gentle smile. When her smile widened, she looked even more attractive and impish.

At this moment they were sitting quietly. I cleared my throat and both of them turned at the same time to look at me. Both had amber eyes. Shalinah's eyes looked watery, as if she was on the verge of crying; Hayati's eyes were bright and smiling.

I asked them, 'When would you like to go home to rest?'

All three shook their heads in unison.

After the casket and all the relatives arrived, everyone returned to the mosque.

The imam said a prayer: 'Allah! Do not deprive us of his reward and do not let us stray, preserve us from painful tests of endurance.'

After hearing his words, I shuddered. Do we have to be tested after Father's death? I looked at Aisha, Shalinah and Hayati. After that I returned to the grave. I felt terribly lonely and bewildered.

I, Ma Zhenyu, had just inherited Father's batik factory, and I had also been given the responsibility of looking after these three women. No matter what came my way, what deprivation or test, I would have to endure it, and face up to reality.

I couldn't help but be reminded then that when Father's coffin was lowered into the earth, one end faced Mecca.

After the ritual was over, we started to make our way home, and the sky was a deep magenta. When I reached home, I brewed a pot of silver tip white tea, and as I drank my tea, I thought about my mother.

She passed away when I was sixteen. I had just finished secondary school and was about to sit for my 'O' Levels. Mother's sudden death affected my results. She had ovarian cancer. She had a very tough time in the final weeks, she lost a lot of weight and kept crying out in pain. I was busy with my revisions but I also spent time with her. The day of my last paper, I found out that she had died when I got home.

Overnight, I became someone without cares or worries. I was freed from the two heaviest burdens in my life at the same time

– my terminally ill mother and the exams. My mind became a blank, my thoughts were perpetually in a blur. After a while, as I slowly recovered from the shock, the positive qualities and good memories of my mother came back to me.

Mother woke me up every morning: 'Yu Yu, Yu Yu, time to get up.' Next, she would place her warm and smooth hands on my forehead and flick my fringe off it. The moment I opened my eyes, the first thing I saw was her gentle smile. This was our morning routine from my childhood to my youth, for ten over years. Even after she became bedridden, she continued to wake me up by calling through the walls from her room.

Mother knew how much I love nonya cuisine. No matter how busy she was at the shop, she would make time to cook for me. Every day after school there would be different dishes waiting for me – assam ikan pedas, or babi ponteh, or sambal udang, or chap chye. She watched me as I ate, not leaving the table until I was done, chattering away about her day.

Mother was a nonya, and I was her only child, so she didn't hold back from showing her affection for me. When I was eight or nine, she continued to smother me with her cuddles and kisses. I enjoyed being hugged tightly by her. Before she fell ill, her body was sturdy, warm, and fragrant with the scent of sandalwood from her talcum powder.

After basketball practice, I would complain that my arms and legs ached, and Mother would give me a massage. She was a tuina expert and she had strong fingers. As she carried on with her expert hands, pushing, pressing, pinching and kneading my muscles, she would talk to me. Ai! I got to taste this kind of deep relaxation from the time I was twelve.

These memories of my life when Mother was alive made me break down into tears and sighs.

On the first anniversary of her death, I went to her grave to tidy it up. I spoke to her about my results, telling her how bad they were, how I wasn't able to join the Pre-U class, and that I was going to

England to further my studies.

In August that year I arrived in London. I stayed in the college dorm and I didn't feel at all like going back home. Father came to visit me once. On that trip he told me he was going to remarry.

He said, 'Her name is Aisha, she's thirty years old, a Malay of Arab descent. She is very fair, there is aristocracy in their lineage. Apparently her mother is part-Chinese. She says her mother's ancestors had the surname Chi. You may think this sounds unlikely, but when I checked the annal of family names, there was indeed a family name Chi.

'Aisha is a divorcee with two daughters, one is ten, the other one, eight. For the Malays, the divorce procedure is actually very simple. Besides, in their district, everyone knows her father, Pak Isa Hassan. The batik factory he founded is very famous. After he died, Aisha's ex-husband ran the place. Nobody expected him to take advantage of his position, but that was what he did. Every year he brought a new wife home, and together with his mistresses, he bullied Aisha and her daughters. The elders at the mosque tried many times to counsel him, but he refused to listen to them. Aisha had no choice but to divorce him.

'I've bought over their factory. Do you know which one it is? It's the one near the airport. I've sold our factory and transferred the funds over to Aisha's factory. We've opened it for people to visit, so as to attract more customers to our shop. Aisha's batik skills are first class. She's probably the best in Penang. There are of course more highly-skilled batik people on the east coast, over in Kelantan and Trengganu, but Aisha says she can get a larger market share by coming up with newer and fresher designs.'

'Father, are you marrying Aisha or her factory?' I fixed my gaze on Father as I spoke.

Father looked stunned and then his features became tinged with guilt and remorse. I didn't think that he felt guilty and remorseful towards me; that was probably how he felt towards Aisha.

After that he showed me a photo of Aisha and her daughters.

'Aisha wasn't happy about her ex-husband marrying all these young and pretty girls year after year. Those girls agreed to marry him because he was the boss of her father's batik factory. Aisha was furious also because her father had left the factory to her. Not only was her ex-husband managing it badly, he was also incurring huge debts. And to think, she had to accept his many new wives on top of all this. This was why she made up her mind to leave him.'

'How did she manage to get rid of him?'

'The Malays are different from us Chinese. The ex-husband has to pay his ex-wife alimony, and everything the ex-wife owns, whether it's before or after marriage, still belongs to her.'

'Why was she willing to sell the factory to you?'

'Her ex-husband was too lazy to bother with retail, so he passed the batik on to us to sell for him. Over time he lost all their customers and market share. Anyway, how much could we sell for him? Naturally we would recommend our own batik to the customers first. Their factory couldn't move their stocks and they didn't have enough funds to buy new materials to make new products. Their business was finished. When I got wind of that, I quickly made them an offer. It was a high price. That's how I became their factory's new owner.

'During our negotiations, Aisha had asked me to retain her and some of their workers. I was aware that these people were very skilful. Two of them are artisans from Kota Semarang. Of course I said yes!'

My eyes were riveted on Father's face. I was trying to understand the connection between him and Aisha. There was nothing wrong with Aisha selling her factory, or her getting divorced, or her wanting to work for Father after he had bought over her factory. But how had all this led to her deciding to marry him after less than a year? That was what made me feel uneasy. I studied the photo.

Aisha was tall and she had pretty features, except her face was a bit narrow. She could be mistaken as Chinese. In the photo she wore a sarong kebaya with a blue print. She was as tall as Father. The picture was taken on Bukit Bendera in Penang. Her two daughters were in it too. Their long hair blew in the wind. Both of them wore frocks, one in yellow, the other, baby blue. The bows behind their dresses were also blowing in the wind. The cable car's wire rope was visible in the background, a cable car moving slowly along it. The light in the photo suggested that it was close to sunset. The sky looked pink.

I placed the photo in a frame. The next day, I accompanied Father to Harrods to get a tea set as a wedding present for him and Aisha. Father could see that I had accepted his decision, and so he didn't mind that I wasn't going to fly back for their ceremony. Perhaps he was relieved, perhaps it would be easier for him if I wasn't there. The following month he doubled my allowance.

In the time after that, I became even more carefree. I didn't feel at all inclined to return home even during the holidays. Sometimes, I bought myself a student rail pass and travelled all around Europe. Sometimes, I flew to America. From London, a return air ticket to America cost only ninety-nine pounds and was valid for a month. For those few years, I had a great time. I applied to be a UK resident and after that came through, I had even more reason not to go home. I could continue to live and work in the UK.

I only felt homesick when I heard that Father was ill. He had written to me and his handwriting had become so wobbly from his trembling hand that it was quite hard to read. He was obviously very ill. He wanted me to move back home. I thought then that the tired bird must go back to its roost. I supposed it was about time I went back, so I packed up my things and returned home.

2.

I followed Father's instructions and took over the factory. Early in the morning I went to the factory office. Aisha had already placed Father's cheque book, the key to the safe, the pricelist of cloths, and information about the different grades of dyes as well as suppliers and order forms from customers and so on, on my desk.

'What are you in charge of?' I asked her.

'I take care of sales at the shop, I supervise the staff and handle queries from tour groups and the boutique. When we have visitors, I conduct the tours.'

'And Shalinah and Hayati?'

'Shalinah is our designer. She's very skilful, she can apply wax directly on the cloth, she doesn't need to make any preparatory sketches. Hayati is involved in the dyeing process. She checks that the colours are sealed, and that the dyes and the wax have the desired effects.'

'Let's go take a look.'

Aisha smiled. The stiffness and awkwardness between us gave way.

I had thought it through the previous night. I didn't care who they were, stepmother or stepsisters, I was going to treat them as friends, otherwise things would always feel awkward between us, and how could we work well together if that was the case? This was the way with most things. If one could look at things from an objective and disinterested point of view, it all became much simpler.

I also considered the worst-case scenario. If Aisha and her daughters wanted to take the factory back, I would let them do it, since they had the ability to preserve the batik tradition and pass it down to the next generation. As for me, I would go into something else. Of course, I would make sure everything was in order before leaving; the longevity of the business had been my promise to Father.

Just then, I was walking towards the factory with Aisha by my side. I addressed her as Ji Ji (meaning auntie), but she was only ten years my senior .

'We will go see Shalinah first,' she said, gazing at me. Her eyes were bright and she looked happy.

Shalinah was working on a piece of black silk, the most expensive material in batik production. She applied wax onto a bronze knife, which she was using instead of a nib pen, and she wielded the knife carefully to create images on the silk. She was working on a phoenix design, decorated with chrysanthemum shapes made with undulating lines. The finished product would be the kind of exquisite sarong worn by a bridegroom from the upper classes, the nobility, at a wedding. It would be exorbitant. Each piece could sell for several thousand dollars, possibly even tens of thousands.

Shalinah's skill was such that she could apply the wax using a knife rather than a nib pen, which was what most workers used. Seeing her at work, I couldn't help but feel nervous that she might make a mistake. Naively, I asked her, 'What if you make a mistake?'

She put down the knife. Both she and her mother broke out in laughter. She replied, 'Nothing to worry about. The pattern is so complex, I can easily make the mistake into part of the design. The reason why batik is an art form is because we rarely repeat the same pattern. Every piece of cloth has its own unique design. This is also why handmade batik is so much pricier than mass produced batik.'

I observed her giving the cloth a gentle shake. The drying wax showed faint cracking lines. They were as fine as frost.

'The lines that appear after the wax dries are like the lines you see in cobwebs. We call this the crackle effect. This is the soul of batik. Last year we went to Yunnan with your father. The Miao term is "guotuo". It means spiral or vortex. In Nanyang, in Malaysia and Indonesia, very few people have this skill. It's easy to produce lines when you shake the cloth after the wax has been applied. But to produce such evenness in the crackle effect isn't easy. It depends on the skill of the person.'

'Can't you make these lines with a knife?' I asked.

'Wax is very peculiar. When you use a knife, the effect can be clumsy and inaccurate. Once the wax dries, it's too late. If you do it before the wax dries, you can only work on one portion, the other parts would have dried by the time you're done,' Shalinah explained patiently.

I regret not being more interested in batik when I was a child. I went to Father's factory a lot but I spent all my time playing. Sometimes I made figurines with the wax. There were times too when I brought the dyes to school and I used them on my classmates' handkerchiefs. They were left to dry on the classroom windows. When the teachers saw them, they were so mad.

Besides, I was Mother's darling son. Mother said that the air was polluted by smoke from the charcoal, that the place wasn't sanitary, that it wasn't a place where I should be spending my time. Every time I went there, I was chased out. Once, I was very interested in the caps, that is, the stamp tools used for batik block prints. I observed how the workers were twisting the bronze into floral shapes. I wanted to try my hand at it, but Mother found me and she scolded the workers. She was afraid I would cut myself and catch tetanus. After that I wasn't allowed to touch the caps and Mother also insisted that we moved house, so that we didn't live so close to the factory.

After I went overseas to study I became even more detached from batik. It was only now that I could get to know it better.

Aisha returned to the shop. Shalinah put down her bronze knife and brought me to see the dyeing process. We saw a group of elderly Malay women engrossed in their work. They were in groups of five, and each one had her own canting with its narrow and thin spout. Beside them were charcoal stoves for heating the cantings. They directed the pointed spouts of their cantings at the white cloth before them as they made wax drawings. They were skilful, their pouring was nimble and precise, and their designs appeared on the cloth with such speed, the lines with such evenness, it was truly breathtaking. Father said that his factory didn't have such skilful workers. Now I understood why he wanted to retain Aisha's staff.

'When these women are gone, there will be no one else to carry on this craft tradition and heritage. Young people these days are not interested in learning batik. I fear that in the future, all batik will be produced by machines,' Shalinah said.

Art is like life. Under certain circumstances, when it comes under threat, when it comes under pressure, even humanity won't be able to save it.

My heart suddenly felt heavy. I looked at Shalinah. Her eyes brimmed with tears. She returned my look. Her hair was in a bun like the other day, but this time she had a silver hairpin in it. I wondered what she looked like with her hair down.

'Let's go!' she said.

I stirred as if I had been woken from a dream.

The worker in charge of making the caps was a man with the surname Long. He was already seventy-two. He was Chinese and spoke Hakka fluently. He was also one of staff from Aisha's factory who was employed by Father. He was making images of dragons, phoenixes, cherry blossoms, chrysanthemums, and clouds on the stamp tools.

'In Yunnan, the Shui use subjects from myths and legends, whereas the Miao prefer flowers, insects and birds,' he said.

'Which part of China are you from?'

'My father says we are descended from the Miao in Yunnan.'

I glanced at Shalinah. Only now did I realise that I was in the midst of batik giants: Aisha, Shalinah and now this Master Long; and there was also Hayati, and those elderly women I had seen with their cantings.

Master Long placed the bronze onto a piece of wood. There was a handle on the wood. Together, the wood and bronze looked like an iron. Beside the workers, there was a cooker for melting the wax. The surface was a sheet of metal and the molten wax lay atop it. The cap was placed on the wax and then transferred to a piece of white cloth. As the print was being made, a lot of force had to be put onto the cloth. The workers were usually well-built and muscular.

The factory produced hand-drawn batik, batik by canting and block-print batik. Shalinah beckoned, 'Come, let's go look for Hayati.'

From a distance, Hayati saw us and waved. Her hair was tied up in a ponytail. She was in jeans and a tie-dye blouse. She was vivacious. On the floor there were jars of dyes: indigo, orange-red, chrysanthemum yellow, navy blue, ink-black and other colours.

'Hi! What are you doing?' I addressed Hayati as if she were a kid.

'I'm supervising the tub dyeing.'

'Where?'

'Look, over here. Kak, be careful, your sarong touched the dye.'

'What do you mean by tub dyeing?' I asked.

'Repeated layers of wax and dye are applied to the fabric, which produces an overlapping colour design. Thin layers of very hot wax will often allow some dye to stain the fabric under the wax, whereas a thicker build-up will keep the dye off.'

'How can you tell what the effect is when the cloth is so wet?'

'Look, we have cloth that's mostly dried over here.'

We went to the backyard of the factory where the dyed fabric was hung. I gasped. 'How lovely!'

The cloths hung on bamboo poles had beautiful patterns. Their designs were fresh, there was elegance and harmony in their composition. The colours were brilliant, captivating and mysterious. Art can truly spirit one's soul away.

'We can achieve these sorts of colours because we use high quality dyes,' Hayati said as she touched the cloths.

'What sort of dyes?'

'As you know, some dyes are made from chemicals, some from plants. The funny thing is that chemical dyes fade more quickly, whereas plant dyes produce colours that become even prettier the more you wash the cloth. Blues become bluer, whites turn whiter.'

'Really? What sort of plants are used for dyes? I always thought that our dyes were made with chemicals.'

'Listen up! Indigo comes from the indigo plant. Yellow comes from turmeric or gardenia seeds. Red comes from safflower, black from the nutgall tree, purple from the borage plant. Aiyah! It was your father who taught me all this. He also said that the biggest production of red is in Sichuan in China, and that the nutgall tree attracts parasites called gall wasps which lay their eggs, causing the tree to form a gall around the eggs. Black dye is made from these galls.'

I nodded as I listened, and it dawned upon me that they had inherited not only their mother's cultural heritage, but also learnt a lot from Father. This must be fate. I myself came from a family with three generations of batik business, and was only now starting to learn about the art. I hoped I wasn't too late!

That night I asked them out for dinner, but Aisha said, 'You are still mourning. It's not right to eat out. Why don't you join us for dinner at our place? I'll cook something nice for us to enjoy.'

It was good of her to remind me.

'I hope it won't cause you too much trouble.'

'Actually, you should move back and live with us. We can take care of each other as a family.'

'If Abang moves in with us, we will have one more person to chat with,' Hayati chimed in.

I looked at Shalinah, who was smiling at me.

'Yes! It'll be more fun at home.'

'Why don't you move in tonight? I'll ask the maid to tidy up a room for you.' Hayati didn't wait for me to reply before running off. It was nice to see everyone so excited and welcoming. I guessed it was also better for them to have a man around. The house was also just beside the factory, which made going to work much more convenient. If anything was to happen at the factory, it would be easier for me to get there in time.

But that night, as I lay on my bed, I began to feel a tinge of regret. I feared that this was going to be the end of my carefree life as a single man.

I looked back on the dinner. Aisha was a friendly and thoughtful host. She kept putting food on my plate. Her manner was maternal but also more; there was something very sweet and gentle about her mannerisms. As for Shalinah, she sat across from me with her head lowered, concentrated on her food. Occasionally she looked up and her eyes were filled with questions as if to ask, how did someone like you suddenly appear in our lives? She was a woman who made me feel breathless. Yet she was my sister, so if there was an opportunity, I would definitely ask her why she had so many questions about me.

Hayati was the rowdiest one at that dinner table. She talked non-stop the whole time. This child, she could have gone to university, but she chose to work in the factory. I thought, should the day come when I step down from managing the factory, Hayati could be my successor.

Something must be wrong with me. Why was I thinking such thoughts? The factory was now mine, how could I even consider giving it up?

As I thought about the long road ahead, the unfamiliarity of this place where I was about to go to sleep, the many things I had to learn about the art of batik, that being at the helm of the factory wasn't as simple as running a business, and also Father's request that I write a book about the history of batik, and the question as to whether I wished to start a family of my own, the many girlfriends I had in the past, thinking, thinking…

I was so tired. But my brain was still wide awake. Not knowing if I was dreaming or awake, somehow I made it to daybreak.

3.

Hayati was showing a group of tourists around the factory. She was introducing them to the process of batik-making. She was speaking Mandarin fluently, that little elf! She could talk about the tools, the dyes, everything.

'It was your father who taught us. He wrote about the batik process in Chinese and we memorised it. He also demonstrated what he meant so as to make his explanations clearer. Hayati began to act as tour guide for visitors when she was fourteen, introducing them to the art of batik. She's very articulate and she knows how to handle all sorts of questions. I don't have that ability!' Shalinah said.

'So tell me, what's the standard of you and your sister's Mandarin?'

'We can show people around, sell things, bargain. If it's ordinary conversational Mandarin, we're okay. We can recognise some Chinese characters, but we can't write. Hayati should be better than me. She likes to listen to Chinese pop songs. She loves Liu Wenzhen.'

'What about you?'

'I prefer Teresa Teng. Her voice is so soothing!'

I was about to say something, but Hayati came into the shop with the tourists and everyone had to start serving them. Aisha introduced me to the tour director: 'This is Mr Ma's son, Ma Zhenyu. He's the new boss.'

'So, about my commission…'

'Ah, I can give you an additional five per cent.'

'Thank you, Mr Ma.'

'Please relay this information to the other tour directors.'

After the tour guide left, Aisha said: 'I'm worried that all the other tour directors will start coming here and the other factories and batik shops won't like that; besides, if we have too many groups visiting, it'll affect our productivity. Hayati won't be able to spend as much time working in the factory, and the other workers will also become distracted.'

'After I've been here for some more time, I can help Hayati. I can describe the production process in English. This should attract more overseas tourists to come and visit and buy things,' I reasoned. 'Tomorrow I will discuss with Shalinah and Hayati, to see if we can produce bedsheets and tablecloths. Oh yes, I remember how Father thought very highly of your batik skills, I think you should mentor our workers. Now that living standards have risen, more people like to wear silk. We can produce more silk products.'

'We will need more capital for that. Silk costs a lot more.'

'We can raise the prices. This will increase our earnings.'

'I didn't expect you to be so interested in our business.'

'I studied Business Administration and Sales at university in England, I should know this stuff. Also, I would like to visit Indonesia and Kelantan at some point, to compare our methods and business models. I also want to visit Australia. I want to introduce batik to them. Their fashion is still stuck in the seventies, and besides their summer is very hot, it's not unusual for them to have forty degrees Celsius weather. The clothes we make should attract consumer interest there.'

'I didn't expect you to have even more foresight than your father,' Aisha remarked.

Whenever Aisha discussed business matters with me, she seemed more conscious of her status as my stepmother and elder. She praised me in the way a parent praised their child. In daily life, especially since we lived in the same house and ate together at meals, she seemed to show more care for me than to her daughters. She often prepared the dishes I loved, and she changed my pillow case and bedsheets.

One time I told her I had a headache and she made me lie down and she applied 4711 cologne to my hair. Next, she massaged my forehead and temples, my nape and the top of my head. I closed my eyes to rest. She was so close to me, I could smell her perfume. It was completely different from Mother's; it was much stronger. I experienced once again the warmth that I hadn't known for years, I had never known before that a massage could cure headaches.

After seeing how her mother took care of me, Hayati whined, 'Ma, I want a massage too. My shoulders are achy.'

'I will massage you later at night.'

'Abang, let me tell you how good Ma's massage technique is. Last time your father also got her to massage him every night until he fell asleep.'

'Is that so?' I looked at Aisha and she nodded, smiling. I had heard before that the Malays had a massage technique that was so relaxing that it easily sent the massaged to sleep. It was like hypnotherapy. Of course I wished to experience this sort of massage and I hoped that Aisha would do it for me at least once.

At night I talked about factory matters with Shalinah and Hayati.

'Of the clothes sold in our shop, how many are made with the cloth we produce?'

'Around thirty per cent, I think,' Shalinah replied.

'That's not enough. We should aim for eighty per cent. People say that our batik is one of the best on the west coast. Why haven't we done more to promote our own cloth at the shop?'

'We can get clothes made by sending our cloth to factories, but sarongs and home and fashion accessories still have to be consigned from elsewhere.'

'No, from now onwards, apart from retailing our cloth at places outside, we should also work with one or two factories to have our batik made into clothes, sarong, bedsheets, tablecloths. We can sell this range of batik things in our shop and also consign them to other retailers. In other words, everything that's in our shop will be made only from batik that's been made by us. Only then can we say that our shop is unique and special!'

'I agree, but this means that our costs will definitely go up, which makes it harder for us to earn profits.'

From Hayati's reasoning, I could see that she had a business mind.

'If we follow Abang's plan, we will be able to promote our batik more extensively to our customers. I do feel that this makes all the time and effort that I spend on designing our batik a lot more fulfilling,' Shalinah said, revealing her strong views on the matter.

'Right. I plan to print some small catalogues with write-ups about our factory's special designs and our dyeing process.'

'Not a good idea. Other people can easily copy us then,' Hayati said, a worried look on her face.

'Don't worry. We have the skills, and we're also innovative. It also may not be such a bad thing to be copied. For instance, if our hand-drawn designs are transferred onto caps, or if we use machines to reproduce them, we would be able to go into mass production, which could increase their popularity. I think that where art is concerned, it's a good idea to expand and get our brand out there.'

I said all this to reassure Hayati.

Shalinah added, 'There's no need to be concerned about imitations. As far as I know, batik artists would never copy other people's ideas. We are all committed to making our own designs, to being creative.'

'But people may take your designs to put on caps, to put on moulds,' Hayati said.

'If you ask Master Long he will tell you that when he creates designs on caps, he doesn't fully follow what has been drawn. He's said many times that he may stick more closely to the drawings that are made in our factory, but when he's given drawings from elsewhere, he will never copy them wholesale!'

'It's true that batik made by machines lack character, whereas the ones made by hand are individualistic. Each one is unique. Until now, I've rarely seen two pieces that are exactly alike.'

This caught my attention. I was reminded yet again that batik was indeed an art we should promote.

'What's most important now is to use only the batik that's made in our factory for everything in the shop. Our products should also be made available in shops elsewhere. Tomorrow I will find a printer for our sales catalogue which will be useful for introducing our batik art to overseas tourists and potential business partners.'

Shalinah and I chose several of her batik designs to be featured in the sales catalogue. I asked her, 'What are the qualities of an excellent piece of batik?'

'First, the design should have personality and flair. Whether the images are of fish or prawns or water or grass, whether they are of insects, birds, trees, or whether they are abstract and graphic, it doesn't matter, but what matters is that the design shouldn't be staid. Secondly, the wax must be applied evenly. When the lines are too coarse or too fine, this will affect the overall sense of beauty. The third factor is the dyes. There must be balance. For some patterns, the colours need to be alluring, but in some other cases, they should be muted. When there are multiple layers of waxing, more care needs to be taken with the dyes, to prevent the colours from becoming uneven, the most obvious indicator of poor quality. Finally, after the dyeing has been completed, the process of removing the wax must be carried out stringently to ensure that the colours are preserved. Every step of the process must be carried out properly.'

She even taught me how to look at the patterns, how to look at the colours. I asked her how to tell the difference between machine-made batik and batik made by stamping.

'Machine-made batik has very neat patterns and clean hues. Batik made by stamping has been made by workers, by them using the strength of their arms and hands to press onto the cloth, and the pattern will have places where the motif doesn't join as neatly, and the lines are often not straight. These characteristics reflect the handmade nature of the batik, because human labour, human eyes, will lead to imperfections.'

This was yet another lesson for me. That afternoon we brought the photos of her designs to the printer. There we also arranged for the copyediting of the content in the sales catalogue which was written in Malay. On our way back, I treated Shalinah to afternoon tea at a resort.

Over the tea, she was again looking at me with doubt in her eyes.

'Your eyes suggest that you have a lot of questions in your heart.'

'I do.'

'What are they?'

'Since Ma married your father and we became one family, you'd never ever come home. Now you are suddenly here, and you've also become so close to us.'

'That's right. I am your elder brother.'

'But I keep finding it hard to accept, how come I suddenly have an elder brother? Why is there suddenly a man in my life?'

'Don't you like me?'

'No, ai! You should be able to tell that Hayati and I like you, and also Ma. I often observe how she's always doing things for you. For instance, your clothes can be ironed by the maid like the rest of us, but she insists on doing it. Why's that?'

'She treats me as her son!'

'I don't think so. I don't dare to say anything to her, she's my mother. Hayati is more blunt, so sometimes she will ask Ma why she irons your clothes, why she makes your bed. These are all the chores of a maid!'

'She's lonely. In the past she used to do everything for Father. He's gone so she has no one to serve. She's made me her target.'

'But even when your father was around, she didn't always iron his clothes or make his bed.'

I stared at her for a long time. Eventually, she said, 'I'm sorry I spoke like this about my own mother. I should focus my energies on my batik, that'll make the fears inside my heart go away.'

'What fears do you have?'

'Me? I don't know.'

'Shalinah, please tell me, I've been living in the same house as you for months now. Tell me what's troubling you.'

'Nothing!'

'Would you like me to avoid your mother?'

'No. She's your stepmother, so it's alright for her to take care of you in this way. It's her way of fulfilling her promise to your father.'

'Shalinah, don't worry, nothing will happen. We will continue to live together peacefully.'

She kept quiet. Her eyes had that same air of doubt and suspicion as before. When I lay my hand on top of hers, it was icy cold.

In this instant, Shalinah seemed burdened with worry, but this morning she was so confident! When she was sharing what she knew about batik with me, her face was radiant. Could it be that art has such power over people? That it could affect their feelings in such dramatic ways?

Life's incessant cares and worries, and the additional factor of my presence, were causing her stress and doubt. I wasn't that different from her. Living with the three of them made me feel as if an oppressive force was hurtling towards me all the time; and yet I could also hear my conscience telling me not to leave them. I was torn.

I could only hope that nothing bad was going to happen.

4.

We drove home along the coast. As we went past Gurney Drive, the lanterns were already lit, and the street food stalls were open for business. Shalinah looked nervous. When we reached home, it was already dark. Aisha and Hayati were waiting for us, they hadn't had dinner.

'You're so late. Didn't you think Ma would be worried?' Hayati glared at us.

'We went for tea. That café in the resort is not bad, next time let's go there as a family for western food,' I replied in a deliberately laidback manner.

'Abang, you had better not go back on your word. How about we all go next Sunday? Ma, what do you think?'

'Let's eat, the dishes have all gone cold,' Aisha said gloomily. She looked unhappy. The four of us began to eat in silence.

The next day I was at the factory doing my rounds when Hayati called out to me: 'Abang! I need to tell you something.'

'What's up?'

'You ah, last night no thanks to you, Kak got told off by Ma.'

'Your Ma scolded her?'

'Ma says Shalinah shouldn't have gone out with you alone. If people saw you, they'd gossip.'

'We went for a cup of tea. If you had been with us in the car, I would have brought you along.'

'You would have asked me to join you?'

'Tell me, how did your Ma scold Shalinah?'

'Ma told her to not forget that you're our Abang, and from today onwards Shalinah must wear the tudung to protect her spirit from corruption, to keep herself in check, so that she doesn't give in to her immoral desires. She must keep reminding herself to preserve her chaste and perfect virtue.'

'How can your Ma force her, it should be up to her.'

'She won't be allowed to wear the sarong kebaya anymore. She must wear the baggy baju kurong and cover her head.'

'Your Ma is overbearing.'

'When Ma gets serious and strict with us, no one can reason with her. She's also very stubborn.'

'What did Shalinah say?'

'She didn't say a thing. She's always been obedient and docile. Since we were little, so many things have happened at home, and now we are experiencing a third kind of family life. We will do whatever our Ma asks us to do, but this time, Shalinah was so upset. Her eyes were brimming with tears, I didn't dare to look at her eyes, because I'd only have to glance at them and the dam would open, and Kak mustn't start crying because once she starts, she can go on for a long time, non-stop.'

'Is your Kak very unhappy?'

'Not at all. Kak is actually the smiley one. She's too kind. When she's designed a new pattern, if anyone were to say something nice about it, she would be super happy. The most unhappy person in our family is Ma.'

I nodded because I agreed with her.

'Ma is often unhappy. Sometimes she takes it out on us. Sometimes I ignore her, and she knows that I'm like a boy, that I won't react to her. This is why she often vents her anger on Shalinah instead. Sometimes she will pinch her quite fiercely, and she'll say she's not allowed to cry; other times she'll scold her but without raising her voice. She grinds her teeth and mutters her angry words spitefully. Once she did this to me, I was only eight at that time and I was so frightened. Only Shalinah can tolerate her.'

'Your Ma is really too much.'

'But after she's gotten it out of her system, she seems to come out of a trance, and she will be filled with regret. Every time she would hug Shalinah tightly and say how sorry she is. Shalinah's eyes would fill with tears but she wouldn't allow herself to cry.'

'I'm going to have a talk with your Ma.'

'Abang! Please don't do that. Just act as if nothing's happened. Don't provoke her, and don't speak up for Shalinah. After some time, everything will be fine. Please promise me, I know Ma better than you, and I am even more protective of Shalinah than you,' Hayati pleaded with me.

She was on the verge of tears, so I said, 'Alright, I promise you I won't say anything.'

'Just listen to me and things will be fine. I know both of them very well. It's best not to blow up the matter, otherwise you can forget about continuing to live with us.'

'Hayati, I didn't realise you could be so mature!'

By now I, too, felt more alert, and I was also considering our lives together in the days to come, so I said, 'In future let's just talk only about work, let's focus on our batik, and make a huge success of our factory. Maybe in the next two to three weeks, after the catalogues have been printed, I'll make a trip to Australia to see if there's a market for us there. I should write tomorrow to some factories in Australia, I should start to make contact with them, yes, let's move on like this.'

The storm was finally over! But I was still worried about Shalinah and I thought I should find an opportunity to see her and ask after her.

That day I didn't see her in the factory. I was busy looking through the factory's accounts and customer database. I also drafted the letters to the Australian factories. It was evening when I finished everything and my shoulders and neck ached terribly.

At the dinner table that evening, I finally saw Shalinah. She was indeed dressed in a green baju kurong, and her hair was hidden inside a tudung. Only her oval face could be seen. I felt a sudden pressure, something which I had never felt before, coming towards me. Rules and constraints imposed by religion can be incomprehensible. I thought about finding a suitable time to speak to Shalinah.

'Today I had to go through our accounts, and also I had to write the letters to factories overseas. My shoulder pain is killing me. I feel like asking Ji Ji to give me a massage.'

'Later on, when you are ready for bed, I will come to your room,' Aisha replied. I averted my eyes from Shalinah. But I knew even then that her eyes were probably filled with doubt and suspicion!

I didn't dare to look at her because I was afraid I wouldn't be able to suppress myself from voicing my views on how traditional and religious values and conventions can be too restrictive. A parallel could be drawn between what Shalinah was going through and what I myself was experiencing. I also had to hold back from following my heart's desire to spend time alone with her because of the values and conventions of traditional Chinese society.

When Aisha's fingers pressed on my shoulders, I felt the tension spread from my shoulders to my neck, then to my chest. She said, 'You have a lot of air trapped inside. You'll feel better after I use acupressure to release it.'

She picked up a porcelain spoon and used it to stroke my back. These acupressure strokes made me feel much better.

After she finished with the spoon, she continued to press on my meridians all across my body. At first I was able to chat with her, and I thought that when she was done, I would speak to her about how she was treating Shalinah, the rules she was making Shalinah obey. But I felt so drowsy because of her firm and gentle hands.

They gave me the sensation of something soft and comforting, like cotton wool, that moved from my neck to my shoulders and back. Just as I was about to nod off, I felt something else pressing on my back. It wasn't her hands. I sensed it was her face, but by then I was simply too sleepy to do or say anything. I fell asleep.

The next day, it was dawn when I woke up and found that I was lying on my chest. I felt energised. Aisha's massage really worked wonders for my fatigue. It seemed to me that her massage technique wasn't Malay, it was Chinese. If this was really the case, then Aisha was not only well-versed in the art of batik, she also knew how to use qigong to press on the meridians. I guessed she must have learnt this from her Chinese mother. It was a traditional Chinese method of meditation that could not only relieve aches and pain, but also benefit a person's health in general. I used to learn qigong from a Chinese qigong instructor in England, so I knew a little about these things. Aisha merged what she knew about qigong with her knowledge of Malay hypnotherapy. Just then I remembered that she had pressed her face onto my back before I fell asleep. My whole body began to tremble, I felt horribly uneasy!

I wanted to look for Hayati immediately, and Shalinah too. I was very nervous.

Just as I opened the door, Hayati was outside and she almost walked straight into me. She looked panic-stricken as she tugged at my sleeve.

'Quick, hurry, we have to rescue Shalinah, Ma is hitting her! I realised earlier on that both of them were not in the house, so I guessed something must have happened. Ma and Shalinah are in the small hut behind the factory. Quick, we must hurry there! Ma hasn't been like this with Shalinah for a long time, I'm really scared!'

We sprinted to the factory. I called Shalinah's name hysterically. Hayati told me to be quiet.

When we reached the hut, we could hear Aisha's voice: 'Why don't you speak up? Answer me, why don't you cry? Since you were little you're always spying on me, why can't you sleep deeply like your sister? Why must you wake up in the middle of the night and creep around the house? Since you were little you've never trusted me, you're always following me around like a spirit. Why? Why?

'I want to strangle you, I want to pinch you, he's your abang, you think I don't know that you've fallen in love with him? From the first time you saw him, you already fell in love with him, you can't hide this from me. Sure, you can marry him, there's nothing in Islam that says you can't, you're not related by blood, but what will all our relatives say? I object, and the Chinese will be the same. Everyone will talk about you two. And besides, he may not love you, he may not want to marry you.

'You spend the whole day together, working on some catalogue, but you can't hide your true feelings from me, I've been spying on you two. You're shameful, you think you can steal him from me, don't you know he's my son, my darling son, he's Allah's gift to me, Allah saw that I have no son, He took pity on me, gave me this step-son, I married his father, and from his father, I got this son, and now he's living with me, he gives me hope.

'He inherited this factory, this is my family's factory, I gave myself and did everything I could to stay with the factory. I can't leave it, this is where we were all born, our ancestors all died here, their spirits tell me to take care of the factory, and I almost lost it, it nearly happened, I almost lost our family's factory, Shalinah, my child, you should feel sorry for your Ma, you should sympathise with her, please forgive me, my pure daughter, forgive me! From last night you've been tormenting me till now...'

Aisha broke down into inconsolable tears. Hayati and I entered the hut. She and Shalinah were in a tight embrace. Shalinah didn't cry, she was trying very hard not to start, and she kept patting her mother's back.

Aisha seemed very tired as she continued to wail and cry. She seemed to have aged many years, she looked like an old lady; overnight she had become so much older than before. I asked

Hayati to help her back to her room to rest.

Shalinah looked at me mutely, her face told me how helpless she felt. I told her, 'Let's go for a walk.'

We went to Tanjung Rhu Beach.

5.

In the morning, Tanjung Rhu Beach was so peaceful. There were no tourists, and the waves rushed to the shore from a great distance. This was the most beautiful place in Penang, I had never seen such a sandy beach, and there were small dunes everywhere. When you put your foot inside, the sand came up to your knee. The sand was cool in the morning, as cool as Shalinah's hand.

We sat down. Far away on one side was the resort. We were in the north, so the sky was a pretty lilac. Shalinah's face, under this early morning light, looked haggard and pale. She began to speak:

'Last night I woke up in the middle of the night and I went to look for Ma in her room but she wasn't there. I went to your room and found her lying on your bed with her face on your back. I was shocked, and also very angry. Thankfully she was only lying there with you. I yelled at her but she refused to move. I walked close to her, and I saw then that she was in fact awake. She stared at me with her angry eyes.

'I pleaded with her to leave your room, to leave you alone. She jumped up and grabbed hold of me and started to pinch me. She also tried to scratch me, so I rushed out of your room and ran to the factory. She chased after me, I knew she was incensed, and yet I couldn't help but remind her of how many years ago, it was after she had given your father a massage, after he woke up, they became a couple.

'She refused to admit that she felt anything other than maternal feelings towards you. What could I say?'

Listening to her, I began to feel my whole body turn cold. But I continued to press, and asked, 'Why did you go to her room in the middle of the night?'

'Ai! Ma is a very weak woman. I remember that when I was six, one night I woke up at midnight and I couldn't find her. Pa was in one of his other wives' rooms. They were all sound asleep. I saw that the door at the back of our house was open, so I ran to the factory to look for her. There I found her sitting by the side of the well behind the factory. She was sobbing. I ran over to her and pulled her away from the well, and I pleaded with her to return to her room and to go to sleep. She hugged me as she continued to cry. Finally I managed to return to the house with her. After I grew older, I realised that she meant to kill herself that night.

'Since that incident, I often wake up in the middle of the night. And each time I would run to her room to see if she's there. Only when I know for sure that she's asleep, can I fall asleep again.

'After Pa left us, before your father came into our lives, Ma had two or three other men who would come and spend the night with her. Each time I begged her to stop. For this reason she hates me, and so she pinches me, she hits me.

'She knew that what she was doing was wrong. Every time I stopped her, she would be enraged like a mother leopard and claw at me, she would attack me, and say she wanted to strangle me. I always remained calm, I think I got my strength from Allah, otherwise how could I be so brave? Each time after she regained her usual self, after her fit was over, she would regret her actions.

'I don't know if what I did was right or wrong. Sometimes I really envy Hayati. She always sleeps till the morning. She doesn't know how the night is full of evil, that night time is when demons come out, that it is when people are tested.'

There and then I remembered what Aisha had said to me the previous night.

'When we got to the factory this morning, I heard your Ma say that I'm her son, that I'm the stepson Allah has blessed her with,' I said.

'If that is what Ma thinks, then that would of course be the best. I hope that she understands from this day onwards that you're her son. I have often thought that she is confused.

'Ma has always been deeply unhappy. There aren't many men left in her family. After my two uncles died, her father passed away and she inherited the factory. Then my Pa made a mess of it, which saddened her a lot. She was always stressed about something: one moment her husband, or else her family, and if not that then, the factory. Anyway, there was always something on her mind, so she rarely had any peace.

'Do you have any idea how tired I am? So tired of facing a mother like her, someone who's so filled with hatred, who's got so many knots tied up inside her, knots which she can't be free of; someone who can kill herself at any time or place, someone who's ready to harm herself, or do something to hurt me or Hayati.'

'I think I should have a good talk with her.'

'That may be our only solution.'

'Shalinah, tell me, do you hate your Ma?'

'I don't deny that sometimes I hate her a lot, especially when she pinches me, shoves me, hits me, but my love for her is greater than my hatred. Do you know how much I love her? She also knows that I love her, Hayati knows this too, but she… she… we… we are…'

Shalinah broke down in floods of tears. She wiped her face with the back of her hand, and then with her palm, with her sleeve, but still her tears continued. I reached for her face to comfort her and a tear as large as a bean landed on the back of my hand. It was burning, and my heart felt a spasm of pain.

'Stop crying, Shalinah, stop crying,' I urged her.

As I touched her tearful face with my hand to comfort her, she tried to catch her breath, gasping, and I drew her to me and hugged her. She rubbed her face on my shirt, and her bun was starting to come loose. I had always wanted to see what she looked like with her hair down. So I removed her hair pin, and then I removed the many clips that kept her hair in place.

All the while my hands were trembling, as if I was undressing her. I could feel her body trembling too.

Her hair fell long and loose around her like waves. Her face looked even prettier framed by her hair. She gazed at me with her eyes still brimming with tears. I smoothed her long hair with my fingers, and then through her hair, I touched her back. Her body began to tremble again. My breath quickened. Suddenly her body made a 'su' sound and she was up on her feet, sending my hands onto the sand.

When I realised what was going on, she was already standing in the shallow sea water. I went towards her and said, 'Let's go back.'

When we got back to the factory, Hayati was listlessly arranging some batik in the shop. I asked her, 'Where's your Ma?'

'She took a sleeping pill, she's asleep now.'

She looked at Shalinah.

'Kak, before she fell asleep she was calling your name. She says you need to rub medicated oil on your bruises, otherwise they'll turn black. Come, let me apply some for you.'

'No need, it's nothing,' Shalinah stopped her.

I caught hold of her, and I rolled up her sleeve. That was when I saw the already-darkening patches where her Ma had pinched her. I was enraged.

'In future if she pinches you, or hits you, I won't forgive her. As for you, why didn't you run away from her? If you had stayed away from her, this wouldn't have happened.'

'Abang, you don't understand our family affairs. Ma hasn't gone insane till now because she can vent her frustration on my sister.'

'If she should use a knife one day, you'd be slaughtered by her.'

'That would never happen, Ma loves us at the end of the day. She is alive because we are by her side, and now there's also you. If she treats you as her stepson and you respect her as stepmother, things will improve.'

'No, when she's awake, I am going to have a good talk with her. What happened last night must never happen again.'

I returned to my room, I looked at my bed and I shuddered. I told myself, I can't live here anymore, I should move back to the small house my mother bequeathed to me. Although it was a little further away from the factory, it was my own home and I would feel safer there. And so I made up my mind to move out.

As long as I moved out of this big house, as long I wasn't living under the same roof as the three of them, there was a possibility that things would become clearer and we might even forget that all this unhappiness ever happened.

I suddenly recalled that there was a framed Quran verse hanging above my bed in my old home which said something like:

'Any of you who does wrong out of ignorance and then repents after that and corrects himself – Allah is Forgiving and Merciful.'

I ran outside and quickly drove to my old home. I climbed onto the bed in my old bedroom and took the verse down from the wall to study it. The verse was Quran 6:54.

I hoped to use this verse to persuade Aisha to change her ways.

That evening, I was finally face-to-face with her.

'Ji Ji, I wish to move back to my own house.'

'What I did last night was really embarrassing,' she muttered to herself.

'I will still come to the factory every day for work and I will have dinner with you all. After dinner I will go back to my house.'

'I didn't mean to act that way. I have no idea how I came to put my face on your body,' she continued to murmur, but this time her eyes were on me.

'I'll continue to take good care of the business, you don't have to worry about that.'

'I wasn't thinking about anything. I just wanted to take a nap beside you, because I'm really so very tired.'

'I've gone through all our accounts, and I'm sure we will do better.'

'Later on Shalinah came to look for me, and I am also not sure why I got so mad at her. With her there, it felt as if the situation suddenly became sinful and frightening.'

'Batik is really an art form. It will stand the test of time. It's truly deserving of our best efforts to study it and improve at it.'

'Shalinah is like a mirror. Even when she doesn't speak, just looking into her eyes, you will see your own guilt. I really cannot stand it.'

'You should focus your energies on batik. You can go back to doing what you excelled at, making batik on silk with stencil and clipboard.'

'I am very weak and many of my actions are confusing even to myself. Only Shalinah can protect me, my poor daughter, she spends more time taking care of her mother than herself.'

'Don't dwell any more on the past. Put your focus on batik. From the melodies inside your heart, whether they're full of grief or joy, you can make new compositions on cloth!'

'I want to teach everything I know about batik to Shalinah, my baby.'

'Do you see this Quran verse? Allah is Forgiving and Merciful. I'm giving it to you, you can hang it over your bed, okay?'

'Zhenyu, you are also my son. Thank you for the verse, I will look at it every day and night. I shall repent and pray that Allah will forgive me.'

I held Aisha's hand and put my arm around her. She will always be my stepmother.

6.

Early the next morning, Hayati knocked on my office door: 'Abang, come and see! Ma is teaching Shalinah. Come, quick!'

I put down what I was working on and followed her to the factory.

Aisha was handling a bale of silk that was between five and ten feet long, enough to make one or two garments. Unlike Chinese silk, the silk used for batik is translucent. When dye is added, it bleeds through the cloth very quickly. Because the fabric is soft and thin, the wax can't be applied using a knife or canting.

Aisha secured the cloth onto a frame attached to a stencil. She began to pour the molten wax into the stencilled areas. Once the wax was dry, she would remove the board and begin the dyeing process. Aisha explained to Shalinah: 'The silk is thin and light, you have to take care not to use too much wax. As to knowing when the wax is dry, that depends on your experience. If there is too much wax, the cloth will shrink, and the wax may even cause the cloth to tear. If the board is removed prematurely, the wax below the surface may not have dried, it would leak and the entire piece of cloth would be ruined. You can stencil all kinds of images, for instance, orchids like Vandas, butterflies, but they shouldn't be too complicated since the silk itself is already a very beautiful material.'

From then on, our factory began to focus on making batik on silk.

We also began to receive orders from factories in Australia. Our business was thriving.

My relationship with the three of them became less turbulent, more peaceful.

This very morning, I opened Father's drawer, and I looked through one of his notebooks. This was what he had written on the first page:

Batik came to Nanyang from Yunnan in China. In the twelfth century, Chinese sailors used the compass to sail the seas, going to distant countries. Many mercantile vessels went to Dongyang (Japan), and also to Xiyang (the lands of the Indian Ocean). This is recorded in *Matters Worth Discussing from Pingzhou* written in the Song dynasty.

The art of dyeing began during the Tang dynasty. In records dating back to the Song dynasty, it is written that dyeing was the specialisation of the Miao, and the dyed cloth were called 'patterned cloth'. The dyeing methods described in *Representative Answers from the Region beyond the Mountains in the South* are the same as that of batik in Nanyang.

During the reign of the Hungwu Emperor in the Ming dynasty, the art of dyeing flourished. In the emperor's fifteenth year, his army invaded and conquered Yunnan. That region's rich folk traditions naturally spread to the emperor's dominion. When Cheng Ho (Zhenghe) was sent by Emperor Chengzu to sail down south, Chinese traders had already established trade routes in the Indian Ocean, and they had brought 'patterned cloth' to Nanyang. Cheng Ho himself was from Kunyang in Yunnan. When he encountered batik, he was delighted to see far the indigenous folk culture of his native land had travelled.

Nanyang was a region known not only for the spice trade. It was also renowned for its production of dyes; Indonesia's Java, Sumatra and the Malay Peninsula were places known for batik partly because of this and also because descendants of the Miao had settled in these areas after they left for Nanyang during the Tang dynasty. Perhaps that was when "patterned cloth" and the art of dyeing arrived in Nanyang.

According to the *Malay Annals*, the earliest 'patterned cloth' in Nanyang had motifs of flowers, phoenixes, dragons. These subjects were not local, but were typical of Yunnan and Guiyang's Miao cultural heritage.

When Cheng Ho was in Nanyang, he visited Malacca and Penang. In Penang's Batu Maung he left a footprint on a rock, an unbelievably large footprint. In the temple close by, the incense offerings never cease. This is what the people in the area believe, and it is possible that this is not entirely superstition.

The batik in Penang and in Indonesia's Surabaya are made using very similar methods, especially in the making of caps and the shape of the knives. Many of the owners of batik factories in Indonesia are descendants of Chinese immigrants, and in their homes, one finds artefacts from the Ming dynasty.

I read up to this part, filled with astonishment by the passing down of cultural heritage.

Laying Father's notebook aside, I recalled what he had said to me as he lay dying: his wish that I write a book about the history of batik in Nanyang. In fact, he had already done a lot of research. I now understood why this undertaking meant so much to him. It was not irrational, so I decided to begin writing.

I still liked Shalinah a lot, but she didn't give me any opportunities to show this to her. Perhaps she didn't feel the same way, or perhaps she behaved this way because of Aisha. She didn't want to hurt Aisha, so she made the decision not to love me. I think she feared that Aisha would be overcome by a deep sorrow.

Now the four of us got on well. They looked after me, and I looked after them.

I recalled the imam's prayer at Father's funeral where he had said, 'Do not let us stray, preserve us from painful tests of endurance.'

In truth, we had all had to go through painful tests of endurance, and in the short span of six months, it was only today that we managed to pass through the valley of death without being harmed.

In the not distant future, I will find a Chinese woman to marry and start my own family. By then I wouldn't be tied to Aisha, Hayati and Shalinah. I shall rely on my own family, and on the magnificent art of batik.

BAI XIANGZU AND HER EMBROIDERED PEACOCKS

The Embroidered Peacocks

WHEN I SAW the ad, my heart felt fit to burst. This is what it said:

> Mdm Bai Xiangzu will be your personal tutor in the renowned art of Chinese embroidery from Guangdong. The course will include the three traditional stitching methods of the Yue School, using threads of silk, gold, silver and other materials. Mdm Bai was trained in a workshop in Guangdong since young. She is a skilled maker of embroidered arts and crafts. Her works have been sold in London, Panama and other countries. This course is an opportunity for women who are interested in embroidery to be taught by an experienced practitioner. To avoid disappointment, enrol for a place as soon as possible.

The ad is dated 1st October 1975. It was placed by Nan Hua Seamstress, a shop situated in Lorong 20 at Geylang.

Bai Xiangzu is indeed still here in Nanyang. I can still remember that year in Guangzhou when she first arrived at our workshop. She was very young, and her sewing was impressive for her age. She was very bright, no one else was her match. Most of the embroiderers sewed according to the drawings they were given. To be able to do this competently, representing with accuracy what had been drawn, was already an achievement. Xiangzu's sewing made the drawings she embroidered seem more lively, more captivating.

When she embroidered flowers, she didn't follow the colours indicated by the workshop's artists. She would play around with the materials she had at hand; in places where the embroidered flowers were meant to be in lighter hues, she would find ways to introduce contrasts with darker shades. She had an excellent eye for colour. Everyone would be embroidering plum blossoms, but once the works were finished, you would hear people exclaiming:

'Aiyah! Xiangzu, you've made pastel green plum blossoms!'

'Look, this is a peach blossom, this gorgeous red is for the red peach blossom!'

'Xiangzu, you've altered the drawing, Master Teacher is going to scold you.'

Red peach blossoms have huge flowers, and these could have variegated and thickly petalled heads made up of two colours, red and white. Xiangzu's embroidered peach blossoms captured the flowers' radiance; everyone else didn't dare to embroider peach blossoms with many petals. Master Teacher, whose drawing of the flowers she had altered, was incensed at first, but then he studied her embroidery slowly, contemplating her stitches, the effect they had created. Subsequently, he brought her embroidery home. Everyone was stunned. As for Xiangzu, she just grinned mischievously.

Something else happened back in that workshop. Something even more memorable. To think of it now, so many years later, still gives me joy.

Traditional embroidery in Guangdong consists of two schools, the Cantonese and the Teochew. Back then, in the Teochew school, the most skilful embroiderers were men, and they were given the honorific title of 'embroidery scholars'. In those days, it was impossible for female artisans to rival their male counterparts, and this influenced how the embroidery workshops in Guangzhou were run. The workshops employed women as embroiderers. Though the women's embroidered works were praised for their level of detail, they fell short of the kind of attention that was manifest in the works of the male embroidery scholars.

Yet everyone was aware that the Teochew school had developed from the Cantonese school. In the minds of most of the people in the workshops in Guangzhou, there was a secret wish for a competition to be held between the Teochew and Cantonese schools. Only then would it become clear which school was superior.

And indeed, that was what happened in 1930 in Jiangnan, when a competition was held and both schools submitted many works to vie for top honours. There were numerous outstanding works from the Teochew school. Despite that, our Cantonese workshop won great praise for the works we sent, amongst them the embroidered peacocks by Bai Xiangzu.

The story of how that work came to be made must be told, as it wasn't a smooth sailing journey for her. The first difficult situation to be handled involved Old Zhao, the artist who had joined our workshop after Master Teacher courted him to come over from Sichuan.

Old Zhao was an artist of Shu embroidery. Master Teacher had met him in Sichuan one year when he went there to learn more about Shu embroidery. Master Teacher was impressed by how realistic Old Zhao's drawings were. Whether he drew flowers, insects, fish, mountains or people, his skill was such that everything looked lifelike. He was able to bring a three-dimensionality to his depictions, something which was absent in the drawings of Cantonese artists. Master Teacher offered Old Zhao a high salary to entice him to join our workshop, treating him like a brother. Soon after Old Zhao joined our workshop, he produced a drawing of peacocks. It was a masterpiece. Seeing that drawing, you might even think it was a waste for it to be turned into embroidery.

When Old Zhao heard that Xiangzu had been tasked with embroidering his drawing of peacocks, he made his displeasure known. Although he hadn't been with us that long, he had already heard our workshop's artists' complaints about Bai Xiangzu. She was notorious for making changes to their drawings in her embroidery. Old Zhao decided to confront Master Teacher.

'Is it true that Bai Xiangzu will be embroidering my peacocks drawing?'

'It wasn't her idea, it was mine. Such a wonderful drawing, only she will be able to do it justice.'

'Bai Xiangzu's embroidery skills are certainly remarkable. She is undoubtedly gifted.'

'I think so too! The moment I saw your drawing, I knew that she would be right person to embroider it.'

'It's fine for her to embroider it, but she mustn't make any changes to my drawing. No changes, not a single stroke.'

Old Zhao's demand put Master Teacher in a difficult position. He knew that Bai Xiangzu's method of working was to go with the flow, that she would allow her needle to take her beyond what was in the drawing as she embroidered. The result was always far more captivating than the drawing. How was Master Teacher going to keep his promise to Old Zhao, how was he going to prevent Bai Xiangzu from altering the drawing?

Old Zhao was a gifted artist, someone whom Master Teacher had managed to poach from his old workshop in Sichuan by using a lot of money and showing him a great deal of respect. Before he came, the artists in our workshop hadn't had any breakthroughs for many years. Old Zhao was able to stimulate them to improve through the work he produced and by giving them pointers. Our workshop needed to respond to the boom in exports, so Old Zhao's arrival was timely. In a short period of time, our artists expanded the range of their subjects from dragons, phoenixes, flowers and birds, to animals, mountains, lakes, rivers, ceramics, and people. The expansion from a narrow range of subjects to such wide-ranging variety was remarkable and succeeded in giving our workshop an exciting new image.

For Old Zhao, and for the workshop, Master Teacher had to keep Bai Xiangzu reined in. So he spoke to her. Bai Xiangzu listened to him without nodding or shaking her head, and then she smiled and brought Old Zhao's drawing to her work area carefully, placed it on her embroidery frame, put on her embroidery robe, and sat down to study the drawing.

As Bai Xiangzu worked on that drawing every day, there would be times when Master Teacher came to watch over her shoulder and he would remind her, 'You mustn't change anything in Old Zhao's drawing. It's such a magnificent drawing, there's no need to change anything!'

If Master Teacher wasn't there, Old Zhao would take his place and issue threats like, 'If you dare make any changes to my drawing, I will resign and go back to Chengdu.'

Bai Xiangzu always kept quiet. In fact, she behaved as if they weren't there, staying placid as a lake. She focused her energies on choosing the right needles and threads.

Master Teacher was beside himself with anxiety and stress from being torn between the two of them.

Old Zhao became far too distracted to make any new drawings.

The two men paced around Bai Xiangzu's embroidery frame every day for several months. All three of them lost weight. You never saw Bai Xiangzu without a needle in her hand and her complexion turned waxy from fatigue. One day, Master Teacher witnessed her boldly weaving a gold and silver thread into filament silk. He lost his temper and yelled at her.

'If you're using filament silk, you should stick to filament silk, why are you putting gold and silver thread in there as well, this isn't how things are done traditionally, this will not work!'

Bai Xiangzu was working on the peacocks' tails, and for the

circular patterns on the tail she had decided to use gold and silver thread. This was going against the traditional method of embroidering such subjects. At that time, there were three kinds of threads that were used in Cantonese embroidery and each of them had their own sewing method. Bai Xiangzu was breaking rules again, so how could Master Teacher not be anxious?

This time it was Old Zhao who could see the effect that Bai Xiangzu was going for with her innovative choice of threads and sewing techniques. Old Zhao placated Master Teacher whilst his eyes focused on what Bai Xiangzu's hands were doing. He behaved like a husband whose wife was in labour.

When Bai Xiangzu finished sewing one tail, she rose from her seat and went to stand at the window, gazing into the distance at the greenery outside to rest her fatigued eyes.

Master Teacher and Old Zhao began to examine what she had just embroidered, observing the tail from a good distance, then going up close, bending down to peer at it from below, examining it with their hands on their hips, looking at it with their heads cocked to one side. Eventually, Old Zhao said, 'Her method works. Look at how glossy she's made this tail, look at it from where I'm standing, look, her stitches for the feathers at the back are so even, so shiny! And the peacock's chest, look at it, her stitches are very tight and smooth.'

Master Teacher stood beside Old Zhao, feeling uneasy. The light came in through the window just then and fell upon the work on the embroidery frame. The art that Bai Xiangzu's gifted hands had produced became apparent: there was evenness, brilliance, neatness, balance, harmony, smoothness, fineness, and tightness in all her stiches. There was absolutely nothing to fault. Most wondrously, she had managed to give depth and volume to the peacocks, which made their image even more vivid.

Master Teacher could see that she hadn't changed anything in Old Zhao's drawing; she had invented her own way of sewing by going against age-old, traditional conventions and rules through her innovative use of threads and techniques.

Bai Xiangzu, ah, Bai Xiangzu, what a genius embroiderer you are!

In the days that followed, the anxiety in Old Zhao and Master Teacher was replaced by admiration. They were in awe of those magnificent creatures: one posed with majestic nobility, another threw a haughty backwards glance, and another strutted with languor, whilst another showed off its tail, fanning it open. Each had its own personality, every one seemed alive.

The moment the work was finished, Old Zhao took his eyes off the peacocks and gazed at Bai Xiangzu, not saying anything, not uttering a word of praise or thanks. Both his cheeks were moist with hot tears. He wiped them off with the back of his hand and blurted out in an anguished voice, 'See what you've done to me, you young girl you, see how you've tormented Old Zhao!'

The embroidered peacocks won a top prize at the Jiangnan competition. It was honoured as a National Treasure and sent for exhibitions overseas. What eventually happened to it became a mystery. Whether it remained in China or was whisked away to Taiwan, or smuggled to London – no one knew. Unfortunately, not even Bai Xiangzu herself had the answer.

I had my reasons for being so preoccupied with the fate of her embroidered peacocks, for being full of praise and admiration for Bai Xiangzu.

The world of Chinese embroidery was just like that of Chinese opera. The boss was the Master Teacher and we embroiderers were part of a big family, with the more experienced and senior ones being called 'elder sis' or 'sister', and I was the one who had taught Bai Xiangzu how to sew. I had taught her since she was little, I had taught her when she was a young woman. I was the one who groomed her talent until she outshone me, I was her Sister Suxin.

She was sent to our workshop at age ten. It wasn't easy for any child of that age to be patient and diligent at learning embroidery. There are so many things to learn, and all of them are not easy:

from threading needles to the eighteen foundational embroidery methods, and if one has time and aptitude, there are forty, fifty more ways of embroidery to learn.

After that, if you wish to learn how to create certain patterns with certain techniques, or how to choose the right combination of colours to suit certain pictures and their composition, and then there's also a dizzying array of threads to choose from, just red alone includes carmine, jujube red, plum red, tawny red, tangerine red, the red like the wen of an oranda with red cap, crimson purple, magenta, pink and so on – enough to make anyone's head explode.

There are a range of colours for each subject. For instance, if you wish to sew a willow trunk, is it going to be a purple willow, or a red bark, or a grey willow, or an olive-grey willow? There's so much to learn, to get things right, one really has to devote a good eight to ten years of serious study and apprenticeship.

Yet I remember little Xiangzu as she had sat before me, her hair in thick plaits, neatly dressed, with clean fingers and spotless fingernails; how attentive she had been, listening, that intelligent air about her. If I taught her a particular sewing method, she would draw it on a piece of paper; if I taught her about a particular colour of thread, she would keep a sample of it, sew it into her note paper and write notes beside it. When it was time for bed, she would bring her notes with her and made sure she memorised everything before falling asleep.

Her studiousness had a lot to do with her father. He was an educated man. He came to fetch her home for the festivals each year. He ran his own school. He was over forty, a sickly man who was always struggling to catch his breath as he spoke, or else he nursed a phlegmatic cough. He often had to clear his throat after every other sentence. There was talk of his being afflicted with tuberculosis which put people off sending their children to his school. Eventually, all his students stopped showing up. After that happened, he decided to send Xiangzu to our workshop to learn embroidery.

She was a bright and mature child. One day, Master Teacher told her, 'By giving all your wages to your father, you are letting him have money to smoke opium. Why don't you keep some money for yourself? In future, this sum could be your dowry.'

She replied, 'Master Teacher, please give me rice and cloth in lieu of cash, and if there's some balance after that, please give me some cooking oil too!'

She was only thirteen that year.

Her father was no fool; he appreciated his clever daughter's arrangement. After Master Teacher acceded to her request, her father came to our workshop with a rickety old cart and loaded it with rice and oil and other sundries to push back home. After one or two years, he looked much better, his health improved.

When she was fourteen, Master Teacher arranged for her to have her own embroidery frame where she would be embroidering items to be exported. Master Teacher said to me, 'Xiangzu is doing so well and she will continue to make something of herself, all thanks to your guidance and teaching, Suxin!'

We, the older 'sisters' at the workshop, knew that we had very little say in the sort of apprentices we were paired with. There were some whom you could teach for many years and they still wouldn't be able to sew a thing, or at best, they made purses and pouches. These were the apprentices who caused you to vomit blood.

Bai Xiangzu didn't let any of us down. She completed the embroidered peacocks, a masterpiece which brought her fame, and for a while, I, too, basked a little in her glory.

Thirty years have passed and now I can hardly believe that I will see her again in Singapore. My heart is filled with happiness. I cut the ad out of the papers nervously and decide that first thing tomorrow morning, I will look her up.

Bai Xiangzu

The year I turned ten, my father said to me, 'Zu Er, sit down, I have something to say to you.' He went on to tell me a story from *The Biography of Lie Chao's Poetry*, about an Imperial Scholar who was an official in Yangzhou. This man played the guqin, he was good at chess, calligraphy, painting, he could write poetry and wield a sword. He was good at everything except for embroidery. So he went to Suzhou to learn embroidery. And that won him praise.

'Do you want me to learn embroidery?'

'That's correct. For many years now, this is an art for ladies.'

'Who's going to be my teacher?'

'I will send you to a workshop in Guangzhou to learn the art. It's the best place to learn embroidery.'

'Where is this place?'

'In Xixiao.'

'Is it very far from where we are?'

'This is why you will have to live there. I'll come to visit you whenever I have time. Every year during the festivals, I'll come for you, I'll bring you home.'

'I don't want to go.'

I started to cry.

'Listen to me, Zu Er, this will be good for us. Your mother died of tuberculosis, and I fear I may have caught it from her. If I don't send you away, you will catch it too. You're still young, how can I let that happen? How will I be able to answer to the spirit of your dead mother?

'There are so few students left in my school. Only one or two. It's impossible for me to make ends meet. You will have meals and a place to sleep at the workshop, and also the Master Teacher said that as long as you learn to sew simple things like pouches, purses, curtains, you will earn a salary.

'This tuberculosis is hard to cure. If I don't arrange for you to go away, it may be too late. I thought of sending you to an opera troupe, but I was worried that you might be led astray or bullied. It's not a good place for bookish people like us. Far better for you to go to an embroidery workshop. Do you know that in Chaozhou, they even have embroidery scholars? Families send their sons to workshops for this reason.'

I understood then that I had no choice, so I dried my tears and asked my father, 'When do I leave?'

'After the Dragon Boat Festival. After you've finished the mourning period for your mother.'

Overnight I became an adult. I quietly packed my things. From my mother's clothes box, I found many things she had embroidered. There were socks and skirts with peonies embroidered on them, there were pillows embroidered with flowers and birds, there were pouches in pretty colours. The stitches were very fine. I remembered that my mother often sewed with a faraway look on her face, as if she were deep in thought. She was good with her fingers; she was a sensitive person. What bothered her most was that she didn't bear my father a son to continue our family name. Before she died, she told my father, 'No matter what happens, you mustn't send Zu Er away to be a child bride.'

My father promised. It was after hearing this that she finally passed away.

On the morning I was to leave for the workshop, I wore a simple floral blouse and trousers. I wore the new shoes my father gave me because they were loose but comfortable.

From our village, we travelled by foot. When we reached Liu Rong Temple, my father hired a rickshaw for us.

'We've already walked such a distance. Why hire a car now?' I asked him. I was obviously complaining. It seemed so irrational of him.

He hugged his bag and looked straight ahead.

'I want the people in the workshop to see that you're arriving in a rickshaw.'

From that moment on, I understood what 'face' meant.

When we arrived at the workshop, I met Master Teacher.

'Show me your hands,' he said.

I held out my hands.

'These are thankfully not the useless hands of a lady. This child's fingernails should be shorter but at least they are neat. These hands look like they belong to someone who is intelligent, willing to learn, hardworking. Their owner is someone who doesn't show her emotions on her face.'

'She's exactly as you say. I didn't know that Master Teacher could read palms.'

'Have you, Mr Bai, taught her how to read?'

'She knows all the words in *The Thousand Character Classic* and *Three Character Classic*. Recently she also read *The Analects* and some poetry.'

'That's good enough. In future, when she's embroidering characters from the classics, I'll explain the background to her.'

'That'll be very good. I will entrust her education to you.'

'Don't worry, Mr Bai, we will not mistreat her.'

After my father left, Master Teacher brought me to see a 'Big Sis'. He said I was to call her Sister Suxin.

Suxin, the Cantonese love the flower by this name. At Zhunan, there is a place called Zhuangtou where many of these flowers are grown. Their fragrance blankets the town like snow.

That night, only Sister Suxin and I were in our room. I asked her, 'Are you from Zhuangtou?'

'Aiyah!' she cried, 'How do you know of that place?'

'My mother told me about it. When she was alive, she liked to wear suxin flowers in her hair. She said that the flowers were sent from Zhuangtou to Wuyangmen Gate early each morning.'

'Was your mother pretty?' Sister Suxin asked me.

'Very! My father used to call her Xiao Nan Qiang.'

'What does that mean?'

'The beauty of beauties.'

'Little Xiangzu, why do you know so much? From tomorrow onwards, I'll be teaching you embroidery. You'll have to slowly tell me everything your parents have taught you. Alright?'

'Sure!'

That night I slept very well. Sister Suxin who took such good care of me also slept in the same room.

Because of Sister Suxin, I began to feel attached to the workshop.

And because of Sister Suxin, people in the workshop began to pay attention to me, and I became more than just an apprentice.

Sister Suxin was an optimistic and happy person. She was ten years older than me. The other big sisters ordered their apprentices around, but she never did that to me. When she spotted a sewing mistake, she would say right away, 'No, no, no, no, no, no, it's not like this.'

A series of no's, speedy and exact, made you put down your needle right away and look at her. She would start from the beginning again, unlike the other big sisters who slapped their apprentices when they made mistakes, causing the latter to be injured by their needles.

She was also the one who taught me about the history of our workshop.

'We're not the only workshop in the city. But we're famous because the early generations of our embroiderers sewed the uniforms worn at the Imperial Court and also the costumes of the emperor's opera troupe.'

Sister Suxin was Master Teacher's favourite embroiderer, everyone said that she had embroidered herself to his heart with the couching stitch. At the time, that didn't make sense to me, but later on, when I was taught how to sew, one of the basic techniques was the couching stitch, a technique for securing a thread over a base fabric by taking tiny stitches over it at regular intervals. I understood then what they all meant.

One night I woke up to the sound of someone crying in the bed next to mine. It was Sister Suxin. I got out of bed, and went to her bedside. I held her hand as she continued to cry: 'Xiangzu, what should I do? Master Teacher likes me, and I like him too!'

'Master Teacher isn't married, you can marry him!'

'But I'm just an embroiderer, he's the boss!'

'Why can't you marry him? He's the base fabric, you're the thread that's attached to him with the couching stitch. From this, a beautiful embroidery will begin, and how wonderful that'll be!'

'Little Xiangzu, if that's really the case, then it'll be beautiful and good.'

'It's possible. Speak to Master Teacher. If you don't tell him how you feel, how will he know what to do?'

'Alright, I'll speak to him tomorrow. Little Xiangzu, you're truly a good sister to me. I'll tell him your analogy.'

Soon after that, Master Teacher married Sister Suxin. At first there was a lot of gossip, but after a while, they stopped. When they spoke to me, they took care with their words. Everyone became very polite. No one knew how lonely I felt.

I was worried that once they were married, Sister Suxin wouldn't teach me embroidery any more. I would have to fend for myself. When Master Teacher asked her to marry him, she was overjoyed and became thoroughly busy with her wedding preparations. She had less time for me. One day, I plucked up courage to speak to her.

'Sister Suxin, you're about to become my Master Teacher's wife. Will you still be my teacher after that?'

'Little Xiangzu, don't you worry, I'll still be your teacher. But wait, with your skills, you should be promoted to having your own embroidery frame. Master Teacher mentioned this before, that back in the Tang dynasty, in Nanhai Province, there was a young girl who was only fourteen when she could embroider seven scrolls of *The Lotus Sutra* on a piece of fabric that was a foot long. You're fourteen this year. It's time for you to do more reading up, to learn more about our art.'

I was given my own embroidery frame, which spurred me to work harder. Thanks to Sister Suxin, I borrowed many tomes about embroidery from Master Teacher's library and developed a deeper understanding of embroidery.

I learnt that embroidery started thousands of years ago. I learnt that the goods we made were sold not only in China, but also in other countries, that they were exported and even sent to competitions abroad. I learnt that apart from Guangdong or Yue embroidery, there is also Xiang or Hunan embroidery, Su or Suzhou embroidery, and Shu or Sichuan embroidery; Guangdong embroidery encompassed the embroidery produced in workshops like ours, as well as that of women at home in the city and countryside, and the Li tribe on Hainan Island.

I also learnt about the complexity and variety of symbols and motifs. The phoenix, for instance, can be represented in a variety of ways. The Hmong are said to have thousands of ways of embroidering the phoenix. Because I was studying and grappling with all the new knowledge I had gleaned on my own, I felt overwhelmed and as a result, I was despondent.

When I returned home for the Mid-Autumn Festival, my father could tell that I was out of sorts.

'Is it because Suxin has married your Master Teacher? Is it because someone fancies you?' He shouted impatiently. I shook my head. 'Then what is it?'

'Because I realised how ignorant I am. Because I didn't know about Chinese embroidery's long and rich history. Because I feel overwhelmed,' I answered indignantly.

My father stared at me. He went to his library and brought me his copy of *The Thousand Character Classic*. He said softly, 'Allow your father to revisit something with you. Do you remember the phrase that comes after "游鹍独运 (*you kun du yun*)"?'

'凌摩绛霄(*ling mo jiang xiao*),' I answered.

'When you were little, I explained this line to you. It comes from Zhuangzi's *Getaway*. A large fish called kun was swimming by itself in the sea when it metamorphosed into a large bird called peng. The peng beat its wings forcefully and with the aid of the wind, it burst through the clouds. You were still a child back then. But you told me you wished to become the peng bird.'

'Now I don't want to be a peng bird. I don't even care to be a kun fish.'

'If this is really the case, why then should you be anxious? In *The Thousand Character Classic* there is a line that goes: "似兰斯馨, 如松之盛 (*si lan six in, ru song zhi sheng*)". When your mother was pregnant, I told her that if the baby is a girl, we will name her Lan, after the orchid; if the baby is a boy, we will name him Song, after the pine tree. The orchid is elegant and pure, the pine tree is hardy and noble. Both are symbols of virtue.'

'Then why was I named Xiangzu?'

'Silly child, Xiangzu is synonymous with the orchid, Lan.'

'I see. I didn't know that Xiangzu means orchid.'

'Yes, because your father doesn't wish that you will become a phoenix, or a peng bird. I only hope that you will remain as virtuous and lovely as the orchid. That'll be good enough for me.'

In that moment, all my cares vanished. I realised that all I needed to do was to give my best to my work and studies, and try in all ways and for all things to stay grounded. This way I would find peace and contentment. I would not lose sight of what is true and good, and I would find fulfilment.

My father didn't stop there. He went on: 'Why not see the kun fish and peng bird as emblems of human thought and aspiration? If your thoughts desire to roam free and far, why shouldn't you allow them to do so?'

After I listened to him, I felt like something opened inside my mind, I had a new way of seeing things, and from that day onwards, I delved even deeper into my studies of embroidery. I became more confident, I didn't feel restrained by tradition and history. I wasn't affected by how others viewed me.

Since I was but a mere orchid, I didn't seek fame and fortune, which turned out to be good for my embroidery as I began to make many strong works. Among them were my embroidered peacocks.

That work, the embroidered peacocks, gave me a sense of fulfilment. Everyone praised it – Master Teacher, Old Master Zhao, Sister Suxin, all the seniors and juniors. It was the single piece of work that affirmed my standing in the workshop.

Life is full of surprises, full of change. One day, when I was twenty, Master Teacher brought a middle-aged man to the workshop. Sister Suxin asked to speak to me, just the two of us. She explained, 'Your father has arranged a match for you. Our visitor today is called Mr Chen. He was your father's student and then he went to Singapore where he is now a primary school principal. He came back to China to look for a suitable woman to wed and your father has agreed to let you marry him. You're not young anymore, it's time for you to settle down. Mr Chen has a brother and a sister, his parents have passed away. His siblings are in Nanyang, and they are both married. He doesn't wish to remain a bachelor. When you are his wife, you only have to take care of him. This can be a good match for you.'

'What about my father? Who will look after him?'

'Mr Chen says he will send for your father too. Both of you will go over to Singapore. He says he's willing to show his gratitude to your father as a former student and take care of him for the rest of his life.'

'I'll have to leave my motherland?'

'Yes, but, Xiangzu, the world is a big place. And everyone says that over in Nanyang, you could do very well by going into business.'

'Didn't you say that Mr Chen is a school principal?'

'Yes, he works in education. Your father is excited about the possibility of a new life. He says that he's willing to help out at Mr Chen's school. Wah, Xiangzu, you're going to be a principal's wife. Come, let us go and greet Mr Chen.'

Sister Suxin brought me to Master Teacher's study. I was introduced to Mr Chen. He had a handsome brow line, his complexion was fair, his laugh hearty. He had the air of someone who loved to read, and was forthright and easygoing. His composure and confidence reminded me of Master Teacher. He had a different aura from my father.

His name is Chen Yongli.

That night I lay in bed, whispering his name to myself, feeling a secret joy in my heart.

A month later, he finally arranged for my father and I to travel to Singapore with him. On the ship, he leaned against a pole and said to me, 'I didn't expect to find a wife who is young and capable like you. Someone who is a skilled embroiderer. Now I understand what it means to be contented'.

The primary school was called Qihua Primary. One morning, I saw my father standing beneath the school bell, looking at the new watch Yongli had given him, grabbing the rope of the bell and giving it a good pull.

Dang dang dang dang, dang dang dang dang!

My father's face was flushed. He said. 'No good, I didn't pull it well enough. I need more practice.'

Yongli stood by the side, watching and smiling.

We lived in a small house behind the school. It was in that same house where my father would later pass away. Not long after that, the Japanese army invaded Singapore. Those were very tough times. After the war, even though life was still full of hardship, we managed to reopen the school as it hadn't been destroyed during the shelling. Chen Yongli did his best to attract students to the school. Whenever he had new resources, he would open a new class. The students reminded me of my apprentice days at the workshop in Guangzhou. Those memories always made me cry silently.

Reunion

Bai Xiangzu wore a pure silk floral cheongsam in pale green with capped sleeves. Her hair was permed. The curls fell on her shoulders.

Many people had shown up to enrol for her embroidery class. She got her assistants to prepare handouts of the schedule for these prospective students. When she looked up, she saw an elderly lady in a floral blouse and matching trousers. The woman looked familiar. Who could she be?

'I'm looking for Bai Xiangzu.'

'I am she, you are... aiyah! Sister Suxin, it's you! How did you get here?'

'I saw your name in the ad in the papers. That was how I knew that you're still in Singapore. I... I...'

'Come, come, let's speak upstairs.'

There was a spacious sitting room upstairs furnished with expensive rosewood chairs. Calligraphy was displayed on the walls. There were many beautiful hand-crafted ornaments with images of flowers, mountains, rivers, fish and so on.

'Do you live here? Where is Mr Chen?' Suxin asked.

'He passed away. How is Master Teacher?'

'Our workshop was nationalised a while ago. Everyone left. Our materials, including the embroidery frames, were confiscated. Master Teacher got so upset he fell seriously ill. Not long after that, he passed away. After a great deal of trouble I managed to move to Hong Kong with my two daughters. There, we did all kinds of jobs. Look at how coarse my hands have become. Thankfully my daughters married well. Since then, our lives have become more settled.'

'How did you come to be here in Singapore?'

'One of my sons-in-law opened a restaurant here. Have you heard of it? It's called Cui Ping.'

'Is the workshop still there?' Bai Xiangzu asked again.

'I hear it's been converted into a warehouse.'

'No wonder! I sent letters to you all but didn't receive any replies.'

'Hai! We lost the workshop, I lost my skills. You've done better than me, you have your own seamstress shop.'

'After Yongli passed away, with my two children studying overseas, I was bored so I sold our house and started this shop. I hired someone to teach me dressmaking, and I myself teach embroidery and sulam embroidery using the treadle sewing machine.'

'Why did you go into making sulam embroidery?'

'It's very popular here. Malay women and nonyas have sulam on their kebaya. The sarong kebaya is very pretty.'

'Yes, yes, and they wear silver belts.'

'A piece of sulam can sell for quite a good price. I provide this service happily. All the women working for me here are sulam embroiderers.'

'Sometimes I look back and think about how hard it was when we were learning how to embroider in our workshop. It was so tough and now all that has gone to waste.'

'Sister Suxin, please don't think like that. If you hadn't taught me embroidery, how would I have been able to make something as great as those embroidered peacocks?'

'So you still remember that work? I was just feeling so thankful that I was supportive back then when you were making those peacocks. If I had hit you or reprimanded you, today you might have chosen not to recognise me!'

'Even if you had hit or scolded me, I would still feel the way I do today. I respect you greatly. Honestly, those were the most glorious days of my life. I will never forget those times we had at the workshop!'

'Seeing you today, I feel really happy. Look at you, you're your own boss now, you've done so well! That year when you first arrived at our workshop, you came in a rickshaw, you were dressed neatly, we all knew that you weren't a nobody. You could read and write, so everyone thought you were the cleverest of our bunch. You were always the one people turned to when they needed to write a letter home or to have a handwritten note sent somewhere. Everyone called you the embroidery girl scholar!'

'Sister Suxin, you're embarrassing me.'

'Who else can I chat about the past with? Everyone else is dead.'

'Embroidery lives on! Sister Suxin, did you know that quite a few of the Chinese families here keep some cherished heirloom pieces of traditional embroidery at home? It's art! It'll never die.'

'Is that so? If you were to give me a needle now, my fingers would tremble.'

'Shall we try? Come, let's go back to the shop downstairs. Come, Sister Suxin, please sew a few stitches for me.'

Suxin followed Xiangzu downstairs. She sat by a table, waiting for Xiangzu. When Xiangzu reappeared, she had a fabric base in her hand. On it was an embroidered peacock. It looked so familiar! Bai Xiangzu said, 'Those embroidered peacocks have been imprinted in my memory. They're such deep impressions that I can easily draw them to this day. I've drawn them as single creatures just like this one here. Sister Suxin, come have a go. Here's a needle.'

Sister Suxin sat down and began to embroider as if she had never stopped. She had no idea that she could still embroider like in the old days. As her hand moved, new threads were stitched onto the fabric, and her tears too, fell on the fabric.

Bai Xiangzu watched her from behind. She sighed, thinking about how passionate the two of them had been towards their art, and how this passion continues to burn in them. It should always be so, and it would be so till the end of their lives!

Those embroidered peacocks, Bai Xiangzu, what a beautiful reunion this has been!

JADE BUTTERFLIES

Prologue

IT HAPPENED when we were still children. One day, Little Grandmother wore her ivory blouse and matching trousers. Her clothes were made of a soft white fabric embossed with tiny green shoots, and they gave one the impression of something bright and breezy, refreshing. Her silver-white hair had just been washed, her hair was wavy, and she was wearing a pair of jade earrings which complemented the pattern of green shoots on her clothes.

She sat on a rosewood chair. On the table beside her were six rose-red suede jewellery boxes, and within each of them lay a jade butterfly pendant.

These jade butterflies had been carved from the same piece of jade and they looked almost identical.

With the wings extended, each butterfly was two centimeters wide and one centimeter long. The features of the insect had been captured down to the feelers, the tail.

A carp was etched on to each of the wings, and each carp had its own fish pattern. In ancient times, pairs of fish and carp signified abundance (the characters for fish and abundance are homophones) and gain or good fortune (the characters for carp and gain are also homophones).

In the light, the colour of these jade butterflies wasn't uniformly green. There were two deep lines of a secondary hue that ran through the centre and through the right side, and they gave the impression of two lively dragons moving in tandem.

Little Grandmother helped each one of us to thread our pendants onto gold chains and she helped us with the clasps too, and as she did all this, she said, 'The six of you will leave me tomorrow when your parents come to fetch you back to your own homes. You've been together for over ten years, so in future you must continue to treat each other as sisters, and no matter where you go, you must always keep these butterfly pendants on your person. Whenever you see the jade, you will remember these times you've had together, and you will also think of me. In future you must listen to your parents, and on Sundays and during your holidays, you should come back here to stay, understand?'

The six of us – Xun Ru, Cai Ru, Xuan Ru, Pu Ru, Jun Ru, Wan Ru – were girl cousins, and our names were given by Little Grandmother.

Back in our room, the six of us examined the butterflies she had placed on us. Then we all discovered that the pendants had four tiny holes each.

'Why are these holes in four directions, up, down, left, right? Isn't this odd?'

'What are these holes for?'

'Why are there six identical jade butterflies? And why do all six of them have four holes each?'

We were puzzling over this when Sister Liu came in. We pestered her for answers. Since she was Little Grandmother's maid, she was the best person to ask.

'Actually, these are six buttons,' she told us.

'Buttons? Buttons made of jade?' Xun Ru was the oldest, she was fifteen.

'Wah, wouldn't that make the clothing from which they were taken from very expensive?' Pu Ru was twelve.

'Has Sister Liu seen that garment before?'

'Of course I've seen it before. These jade butterflies came from a traditional Chinese jacket.'

'A traditional jacket with jade buttons sounds old-fashioned. If it were mine, I would never wear it.'

This was said by Cai Ru, she was fourteen, and out of all of us, she was the best at dolling herself up.

'What do you children know? Men's jackets usually have wooden buttons. The man would wear a singlet inside the jacket, the jacket would be made of silk or cotton. If the jacket was a noble indigo, matched with jade buttons, the overall effect would be very dashing…'

Before Sister Liu could finish, Cai Ru interrupted her.

'I get it, Sister Liu, so what happened to the jacket?'

'It's disintegrated, so that's why these jade buttons were removed from it and turned into pendants and given to you.'

'I've never seen Grandfather before. I wonder what he looks like in a jacket.'

'Your grandfather wouldn't wear these sorts of jackets. He was a scholar.'

'Are you saying that the jacket wasn't our Grandfather's?'

'Then who did it belong to?'

'Was it Grandmother's brother's jacket?'

'Your Grandmother didn't have any brothers,' Sister Liu said. Everyone started talking at the same time:

'Little Grandmother used to be in an opera troupe. She played lots of roles. Maybe the jacket was one of her costumes.'

'Little Grandmother would have looked very handsome when she cross-dressed.'

'Very likely, we see this in the opera all the time, Hua Mulan dressed up as a man, didn't she?'

'But this jacket had six buttons. Little Grandmother is so short, why would she need six buttons?' Xun Ru asked curiously.

'This jacket was taken out of a chest by your Little Grandmother after Grandfather passed away. She often draped it over her shoulders at night. She did that for twenty years.' Sister Liu seemed to know a lot more than what she was telling us.

Who was the owner of the jacket?

We started making all sorts of conjectures and we went on like this until it was very late at night and still we didn't know the truth. The little ones went to bed.

The next day, after breakfast, our parents, our uncles and aunts, arrived to fetch us to our respective homes. After we left, the only people in the house were Little Grandmother, Sister Liu and Uncle Ding.

1.

I finally gave the jade butterflies away.

I am conscious of how little time I have left, so rather than hanging on to those jade buttons, why not make them into pendants for my granddaughters. Maybe one day he will see one of the girls wearing them, and maybe he will find out about me from them. That's one way of giving myself some peace.

What a fantasy!

I could have given the buttons to the First Wife's daughters-in-law, but I preferred to give them to their children, since I had taken care of these six girls since they were born. I had guided them since they were little, I had given them their names after a lot of thought.

After Old Master passed away, I went into mourning for three years. After that period came to an end, I took the jacket out from the bottom of a chest. After I draped it over my shoulders, tears began to fall.

I no longer miss Old Master. Instead, the person who has always been hidden inside my heart resurfaced in my mind, and it is this person whom I miss.

His name is Wu Yu.

The Wu family belonged to the powerful and affluent Cohong in Guangzhou. They were as wealthy and powerful as the Pan family and the Liang family.

Guangzhou's Cohong represented the Qing dynasty in all its trade relations with the outside world. The Cohong was half-administrative and half-commercial in its operations. It was in charge of exports and it was also the authority over foreign countries and companies who came to trade with China. For this reason, it received funding from the Qing government, although in financial matters, the Cohong had a strong advantage in taxes, tributes and even the lottery. They were granted power and privilege by the Qing government over trade matters, which meant they had monopoly over China's trade.

They set up the Thirteen Factories for foreign traders, the Tai-Pans. The activities of the Tai-Pans were supervised by the Cohong.

The Tai-Pans lived in the Thirteen Factories. These were not palatial residences. Usually, the first floor was the warehouse, the office, reception and dining areas were on the second floor, and the third or fourth floor served as the living quarters of the Tai-Pans, their families and servants. There was a stark difference between these homes and the homes of the families in the Cohong.

The Opium War had affected the fortunes of the Cohong. Their offices and warehouses in Guangzhou were either burnt down or destroyed. But these families still had their lucrative trade monopolies.

The Wu family continued to thrive from their trade in arms and grain from the end of the Qing dynasty to the start of the Republic of China. In Guangzhou, they did better than survive – they were vultures in the midst of war and disorder.

Back then, our business in tea, the Tang family's business, relied heavily on their support. Old Master Tang and his men moved tea from south of the Yangtze River to Guangzhou, and from Guangzhou, the tea was exported by the Wu family to Europe and Nanyang.

I accompanied Old Master Tang when he did business in Guangzhou and he would bring me along with him on his visits to the Wu family residence.

Their big house had marble flooring, and sandalwood walls. Everywhere there were antiques on display. There were clocks and oil paintings on their walls.

They had European sculptures in their garden, and a stage for opera performances during the festivals. The Wu family had around fifty or sixty members and the wives and concubines took lessons in singing Chinese opera. I hadn't been with Old Master Tang that long. I had grown up in a troupe, and when I visited the Wu's, I would teach them for fun. When Old Master Tang was away in Jiangnan for work, I visited them because I was bored.

Later on, when Old Master Tang heard that I was teaching them Chinese opera, he was very unhappy. He no longer allowed me to go to their place. He was worried that they would look down on me.

Wu Yu started noticing me from that time.

Wu Yu had a concubine who used to sing Peking opera. We called her Small South Strong. She and I became good friends after she heard that I used to sing Cantonese opera. We were close in age. One day she asked me to her room, and there we chatted about the roles we had played before. She complained that the biggest star of Peking opera, Mei Lanfang, made it impossible for the younger artistes to shine. I realised then that our experiences were very similar. She also talked about how the inflections in Cantonese opera were derived from Peking opera and asked me if I minded her mentioning this.

'I don't mind at all. You're far more knowledgeable than me.'

'When we talk, I also feel that you know a lot. To tell the truth, we were both from opera troupes, so of course we would know a lot more about opera than the ladies in our families. How does your Old Master Tang's First Wife treat you?'

'Quite good. What about yours?'

'Me? As you know, I don't know how to flatter people. I come from Peking opera in the north, but even if I were the Hua Dan, the leading lady, it wouldn't mean a thing. And I just don't like the southerners, especially the ladies who give themselves so many airs and order the concubines and maids around. I treat these high-and-mighty types as trash.'

I could never win an argument over her. I could only feel sorry for her, for it was clear to me that things were not going well for her. She noticed that I wasn't saying anything, so she said, 'Don't worry about me. Come, sing a tune for me, choose one that's really difficult to sing and give it your all. Oh, I meant to ask you: are you from the east or west pack in Cantonese opera?'

'East. I was told by my teacher that we use the huqin and the yueqin more.'

She suggested two tunes for me to sing. I looked at her, feeling as if we were somehow related. My eyes filled with tears and I began to sing. When I sang a verse about how the paper, ink brushes, ink and inkstone were reminders of the scholarly lover who didn't return, about the heartbreak of the forsaken beloved, both of us were in tears though I was still trying to sing. Suddenly we heard someone yelling: 'Stop singing!'

That was Wu Yu. He was in an indigo jacket, and he looked furious, sympathetic and anxious at the same time.

'I thought the two of you sang for enjoyment. How did singing a bit of opera lead to all these tears?'

'All of you think that opera is fun and entertainment. You don't realise that our singing comes from our hearts.'

Small South Strong passed me her handkerchief after she used it to dry her tears.

'So the two of you went from singing together to crying together.'

'So what? I've been with you for four years, only now have I met someone who truly understands me.'

Small South Strong stood up.

'Oh! So I'm not your best friend. Auntie Feng here is the only one who knows you.'

'Of course you are, otherwise why would I have left everything back up north and followed you here? But you're not always with me, and the people in your family are not nice to me. You should be like Old Master Tang and let me accompany you on your trips. Look at how well Fengci is treated by her in-laws. No one bullies her.'

'It's not the same. Old Master Tang has to travel to make sure his goods reach us, and we have to stay put in Guangzhou, our base, to make sure the goods get exported. How can we travel?'

'You always say you can't travel. How about going around our city then? Take us to the flower market.'

I often spent time with the two of them out and about in Guangzhou. During autumn, the flower market was full of chrysanthemums. According to the herbalist Li Shizhen, there are nine hundred types of chrysanthemum. Wu Yu said there should be around two thousand in China, though he felt sure that there might be even more. We joked that he was making this up. He went on talking about chrysanthemums: 'The small ones come in different shapes, and the big ones too. Their shapes are named after other flowers: plum-blossom shape, jasmine-flower shape, osmanthus-flower shape, lotus-flower shape, peony shape and so on. There are many others whose names I can't pronounce.'

'We know all this.'

He went on talking about the differentiations in the flowers' colours, the different kinds of chrysanthemums that were brewed and drunk.

'Enough, enough, look at how bored Fengci looks. I am bored by you too. Let's take the car to Zhuangtou to see suxin jasmine flowers.'

'I gave you the name "Small South Strong" because of your love of suxin jasmine.'

'Master Wu, please explain the significance to me,' I said.

'During the era of the Five Dynasties, the Southern Han dynasty ruled over one of the Ten States, and in the region of Guangyue, the most fragrant flowers were the two kinds of jasmine, suxin hua and moli hua. When the ambassador and his entourage from the Central Plain visited the Southern Han dynasty court, they were presented with suxin jasmine, and the flower was given the honorific name of "Small South Strong", signifying its being the most beautiful flower of that court.'

I understood what Wu Yu was trying to say. Immediately I said to Small South Strong, 'You came down south and you were treated with honour like that ambassador and his men who visited the Southern Han dynasty court. Your name reflects this, Wu Yu does treat you very well indeed.'

'In his household I am definitely the greatest beauty of all. Have you not seen how much make-up those women slap on their faces? How can they compare…'

'Look at you, are you not afraid of being laughed at? Auntie Feng here can definitely compare with you!'

Wu Yu was looking at me as he spoke.

I hurriedly said, 'No comparison at all! Look at how beautiful Small South Strong looks in her ensemble today.'

'Fengci, you wouldn't be saying this in front of your Old Master Tang, I'm sure! We each have our own strengths. But Fengci, I hope you won't be offended when I say this. I think you're too gentle. People will take advantage of this if you're not careful.'

She was right about that.

Then again, her own fate was worse than mine.

2.

Since Old Master Tang forbade me from going to the Wu residence, Small South Strong began to spend a lot of time at our tea shop chatting with me. Every time she came, Master Wu would come to fetch her home when it was time for her to leave.

When Old Master Tang's First Wife fell ill, I had to return to Huizhou with Old Master Tang. In Huizhou I took over First Wife's duties, supervising the servants, taking care of her six children. For two years I didn't see Small South Strong. One day, a relative of Master Wu's rushed to Huizhou from Guangzhou with a message saying that Small South Strong had fallen critically ill. She wanted to see me for one last time. Old Master Yang gave me permission to go. The next day I went in the relative's car to Guangzhou.

When I saw her, I was immediately shocked and afraid. Her pretty face was bloated and swollen. Her complexion was swarthy.

'What happened?'

'His First Wife did this to me. Master Wu is furious. I've been poisoned with calomel.'

'How did it happen? Calomel can be taken without causing such harm.'

In the troupe we learnt a bit about traditional Chinese medicine. Calomel could be mixed with clam powder and plaster to treat acne. It can also be ingested when it is combined with rhubarb, morning glory, coriander flower and so on, as a purgative. It can also be good for the complexion.

'I do occasionally take some calomel mixed with other ingredients as part of my skincare routine. The First Wife must have gotten someone to increase the dosage of the calomel, to poison me.'

'Are there any eye witnesses?'

'Yes, her servant, that young girl Xiao Lan has confessed. The First Wife returned to her family a few days ago. But they deny that she's gone back to them. At Suzhou, where her sister lives, we couldn't find her because she escaped before Master Wu got there. What can he do? She's his wife. Is he going to report her crime? There's so much chaos outside now, who's going to take this case? Anyway, I'm not dead. Fengci, I'm telling you now, if I become a ghost, I'll take revenge on the people who did this to me.'

'What did the physician say?'

'He says I have acute nephritis. Do you know what causes nephritis? It's due to excessive calomel. The western doctor diagnosed this.'

'Is there a cure?'

'My kidney is gone. Master Wu kept this from me, but I overheard him telling his sister-in-law. Look at my body, how black and swollen it's become.'

'What did Master Wu say?'

'He said he will make sure someone pays for this. Early this morning he left for Suzhou to bring the First Wife back. Fengci, he still loves me. He's so sad, he kept crying, saying how much he regrets bringing me to his home, that if he hadn't done so, he could still have come to look for me in Beijing. He did it for his own convenience. He says that his selfishness has hurt me. Sometimes I think I should just give up.'

'Small South Strong, no, I think you should tell me your real name now.'

'My name is Suhui, Fengci.'

'Are you really ready to say it's all over? Suhui, my dear sister.'

'I wasn't ready before, but now that I've seen you, I'm ready. I feel like we're related and you care about me. I am worried about Master Wu. He doesn't tell his wife anything. Whenever he has something on his mind, he'll confide in me. Once I'm gone, he'll have no one to talk to. It's too bad that you're already with the Tangs. Otherwise I'm happy to let you have him.'

'Sister Hui, you shouldn't talk like this. Master Wu isn't yours to give away.'

Both of us hugged and sobbed after this.

The next day Master Wu returned from Suzhou with his First Wife. He brought her to see Small South Strong. The woman shrieked when she saw Small South Strong.

'I'll give you anything you want, don't haunt me! I beg you, I didn't mean to hurt you. I just wanted to teach you a lesson for taking Master Wu away from me.'

'Master Wu, please leave the room. I want to speak to her on my own. Alright, if you're worried, then let Fengci remain, but the rest of you, please go out.'

Master Wu looked helplessly at me. Everyone left the room. I left the door slightly ajar so that he could hear what was being said inside. Small South Strong said to the First Wife, 'Let me tell you this. After I die, I will become a ghost and follow you around.'

'Please don't do that, I'll give you anything.'

'Alright. I want to be First Wife. Will you let me have your title and your position?'

'Yes, I give it to you. Just don't become a ghost.'

'Fengci, do you hear that? Isn't she more pitiful than me?'

'Sister Hui, you should be placated now. It's time for you to get some rest.'

'First Wife, you come over here. Yes, don't be scared, I'm not dead yet, come, let me tell you, I don't want your title and your position. And I won't turn into a ghost, so you don't have to be afraid. I'm going to become suxin jasmine, I wish to become truly Small South Strong.'

Small South Strong was indeed my good sister. She had such courage.

She died in Master Wu's arms. I envied her that the most. Who will be holding me in their arms when I die? I will probably die alone in my bed!

Small South Strong's grave was covered with the suxin jasmine plant when I visited. Her tombstone had lines from the famous poem about the suxin jasmine by the Lingnan poet Qu Dajun carved on it.

3.

After Small South Strong died, I returned to Huizhou stricken with grief. I felt as if I had lost a close relative. Master Wu drove me to the east of the Yangtze River and arranged for someone to accompany me on the boat home.

On the road, Master Wu talked a lot, and everything he said concerned Old Master Tang.

'Did he tell you that the Tang family business isn't doing so well?'

'No. These past two years he's rarely at home. Even when he's not on one of his trips, he comes home at dawn. Is our business in trouble? Can you help him?'

'I can't do much. Our business is shared among us brothers. I don't have much say. Times are very bad. There is chaos outside. With the revolutionaries demonstrating everywhere, it's hard to run a business. There's no more export trade. We are eating the grain we have saved.'

'Is it really that serious?'

'How is Old Master Tang's wife? Is she recovering?'

'Not really. She was very plump before, now she's become thin, and her temper is worse too. She misses her eldest who is away in Shanghai. The younger kids are too young. They cry all day long.'

'It must be hard on you. But you are still lucky, to be with a good man like Old Master Tang. When he was alive, my father spoke highly of him. He said that there were few men who were as trustworthy as your husband and that we should always do business with him.'

'If he weren't a good man, I wouldn't have agreed to be with him. He's old enough to be my father!'

Master Wu gave me a look. I realised he was wearing an indigo jacket. I also noticed that the buttons were made of jade. They were butterflies.

'In future, should you or anyone in the Tang family need

anything, you must let me know. I promise to do what I can to help you.'

Little did I know that this promise of his would indeed come true one day.

When I reached home, Old Master Tang's things were packed. He was planning a long trip faraway. He asked me about the funeral, who attended it and who didn't. I wanted to ask him about his business, but he insisted on talking about household matters, the money that had to be sent to his son in Shanghai, the daughter with measles, medication for his wife. There wasn't enough money to hire the part-time helpers, he wanted me to ask them to stop coming.

He talked in a great hurry. Before settling all the details, he was out of the door, leaving me to deal with his big family and all its responsibilities. I was thrown back into my harried lifestyle again.

After seeing how ill Small South Strong had been, when I saw Old Master Tang's wife this time, I felt really sorry for her. I forgave her for all the unkind things she had said and done to me in the past. I told her, 'Mrs Tang, you must get well. This family needs you. Since you can't eat, would you like a bowl of soup?'

'Fengci, tell me. Are things very messy outside? What was it like in Guangzhou? Were the revolutionaries there?'

'Yes, Guangzhou was in a mess. Foshan was chaotic too. There are revolutionaries here in Huizhou too.'

'Will we be in trouble? Come, help me, I want to go to Old Master Tang's room. He didn't give me the key to his safe. Did he give it to you?'

'No, Mrs Tang, he really didn't give it to me.'

'Has his business failed?'

'I don't know. These few years I've been at home all the time. I'm not sure what's going on outside.'

'We're finished, we're definitely finished. Fengci, listen to me. No matter what happens outside, my children, my poor pitiful children, you must look after them in the coming days. Did you hear me? I paid for you to leave the opera troupe. Who could have foreseen this? This is fate. You came to our house, I let you have Old Master Tang, now the house is yours and my children too will be yours. The Tang family needs you now. You must take care of my children, watch them grow up. Call them to come here now. I want you to send someone to Shanghai to bring my sons Borong and Zhonghao home. I want them to call you Ma, I want to hear this, I want them to acknowledge you in front of me.'

The four little ones who were at home were all called to gather around her. One boy and three girls – she made them call me Ma. In a few days' time, she passed away. The two older boys got home too late. To this day they still address me as Auntie.

After her funeral, it was as she had predicted. The Tang family business collapsed and the extended family dispersed.

We learnt that Old Master Tang had joined the revolution to save China. He sold the Tang family's tea brand to raise money for the revolution. In recent years, he had been helping Mr Sun on his travels all over China. Old Master Tang was even travelling to Nanyang to collect the money that the diaspora, the huaqiao, had raised for Mr Sun and his cause. He said he had to go and off he went. He didn't seem to care that things were very chaotic and dangerous outside.

I wasn't able to accept what had happened to our family's finances because everything happened too suddenly. My servant Ah Liu went to the market and no one would accept payment from her. They shoved the best cuts of meat and vegetables into her basket, and even asked when would we be leaving town. Ah Liu was shocked into silence. She came home looking as if she was about to faint any time.

On the day before he set off for Nanyang, Old Master Tang was calm. He said everything had been arranged.

'I can't continue in Guangzhou, it's not safe for me. If I don't leave, I'll be caught. I bought a stone house in Yuan Lang in Hong Kong. Tomorrow Old Ding will take the two older boys there via the Long Gang route. You and the smaller children will travel there via the east of the Yangtze River. First you will reach Guangzhou, and from there you will take the train to Hong Kong. I'll have someone called Fifth Brother bring the train tickets to you. He will make sure you arrive safely in Hong Kong. It's better not to pack too many things.'

After Old Master Tang left, I dismissed most of the servants. Uncle Ding took the two boys with him. Our house would be handed over to its new owners in two days' time. I packed some money and jewellery, and waited for the man called Fifth Brother to come and collect us. I was feeling out-of-sorts when Sister Liu came to look for me, saying, 'Someone called Fifth Brother has arrived. He says we're to leave for Guangzhou with him.'

I never expected that the person Old Master Tang had referred to as Fifth Brother was in fact Master Wu. Tears streamed down my face as I ran outside to greet him. I was crying so hard I couldn't speak.

'Don't worry, everything's been arranged!'

I was still speechless, but I did immediately feel better, knowing that here was someone dependable who had come to our aid. Master Wu looked around and said, 'We will need to bring Mrs Tang's tablet with us, and this Guanyin idol too. Those scrolls need to be rolled up and packed. Are there any valuables in the study?'

I brought him to the study. Master Wu told me, 'Old Master Tang has left some antiques with me. After you've settled down, I'll return them to you.'

In the study he opened the drawers of Old Master Tang's desk. He took some seals out. He also found a few precious stones, two or three of them were bloodstones. He wrapped them up and packed them inside our suitcase.

The old servants carried our luggage to the bank. As we said our goodbyes, some of them prostrated themselves on the ground. They did this for Mrs Tang. She had taken care of them for many years.

The boat sailed down the Yangtze River. I turned to Master Wu.

'I didn't realise you were the one Old Master Tang had approached to help us. We are indebted to you.'

'I'm just doing what I can. We can't do anything for the revolution. Our ancestors are part of the establishment, we can't possibly go over to the other side. Old Master Tang is different, and besides, he is our family friend. We will do our best to help him for sure. You and Small South Strong were very close. This is also my way of honouring my promise to her.'

'I'm really grateful to you.'

'Old Master Tang has taken care of everything. Don't you worry, once you reach Guangzhou, the situation will improve. I know the place, my people are there. I will accompany you all the way to Hong Kong.'

'If I had known all this, I would have kept the two boys with us.'

'It's safer for them to follow Uncle Ding. The kids with you are much younger, it's better for them to take the train. Old Master Tang said that if I take you to Hong Kong, no one will be able to tell that you and the children are not from my family since we have so many concubines and children.'

He walked away after he finished.

There was a feeling of warmth in my heart. I was relieved to have a good friend like him, especially in such dire times.

4.

When we reached Yuan Lang, I saw the stone house and felt immediately comforted by its sturdy appearance. Although it wasn't large, it would be our sanctuary, a place where we could settle down. With Mrs Tang gone, and Old Master Tang absent, I was head of our household for a change. I welcomed the opportunity and the responsibilities.

Master Wu brought my old teacher from the troupe to see me. The first thing he said was, 'What I said to you before, those words still count today! Make yourself comfortable here. I will help to make the necessary arrangements.'

What he was referring to was the promise he had made years ago: if anyone in the Tang family were to bully me, I could go back to the troupe any time. He would always have a bowl of rice for me.

Not long after, my old teacher indeed found me a job as a seamstress for the troupe's costumes.

In the twenties and thirties, Cantonese opera was at its peak in Hong Kong, and the costumes worn by our artistes had to be well-made. Since I had grown up in the troupe and could read scripts, I was able to visualise the best ways to dress different characters. I could also easily design matching headgear and footwear for the cast.

I became known for my skill and imagination. From the boss of the troupe to the actors and actresses, everyone showed their respect for me by addressing me as Auntie Feng. I was offered front row tickets to every show.

And so our life became peaceful.

One day Master Wu came to see how I was doing. I noticed a tear in the sleeve of his indigo jacket.

'Let me make a new one for you. We can use the same jade butterflies on the new jacket.'

He removed his jacket slowly and handed it to me. He gazed at me and said, 'Fengci, are you happy here?'

'Things are so much better now!'

'I am referring to how you feel inside. Have you thought about yourself?'

'What's there to think about? Old Master Tang will return one day, his children are all here with me.'

'Do you miss him? Are you with him because you feel indebted to him, because they bought you out of the troupe? If I had seen you back then, I would have done the same for you.'

'We are not goods. Buy us out? You think you have so much power. If we don't agree, you won't be able to buy us out either. And don't you dare insult my husband. I used to think highly of you. Now that you've said these words, you've upset me.'

I wasn't sure why I was so angry with him.

'I'm the one who's upset for you. My situation with Small South Strong and yours – there's a world of difference. When we got together, I was in my twenties. When you got together with Old Master Tang, he was old enough to be your father.'

'Don't you dare insult Old Master Tang. I followed him willingly.'

I will never allow anyone to be disrespectful towards Old Master Tang because that is the same as letting them insult me. Why was Master Wu saying these things? Who did he think he was helping? I stared at him. Was he so determined to argue with me? He spoke again.

'You should keep an open mind. Maybe something better will come your way.'

'So what if something better does come along? Before she died, Small South Strong said she was willing to let me have you. She was worried about my future. But I told her not to speak like that, I said to her, he is not yours to give away.'

'Why not? I'm not yours or hers. Who I would like to be with – I myself can decide.'

'But can you have what you want? And what you do not wish to have, can you put that aside so easily? Put another way, what you wanted was what you got, but could you keep it safe forever? Small South Strong is a good example. You loved her so much, but you failed to keep her safe.'

After I finished, he looked at me for a long time. Then he hung his head and left.

Where had my courage come from, to say all those things to him? I had no idea. I was so candid, so forthright. Could it be that there was a grudge buried inside my heart? His words had caused the hidden wound to surface and I couldn't suppress it.

He probably thought, *Since she is so loyal to Old Master Tang, let her remain forever with him.*

He probably thought, *Old Master Tang will eventually return, who am I, I'm just the friend providing some help when it's needed.*

He probably thought, *Since she doesn't fancy me, why should I be upset over her?*

As these thoughts swirled in my head, I couldn't concentrate on sewing his jacket and pricked myself with the needle a few times. Each time that happened, I pressed my blood into the indigo cloth. It blended into the weave. Unless you looked carefully, you couldn't see the blood stains.

For a long time after that, Master Wu didn't visit us. In the past, whenever he came to see us from Guangzhou, he would bring us some preserved mustard greens and some waxed meat. We wouldn't have finished what he had brought on his previous visit when he would call on us again, and so we would always have fresh supplies. But now, we had run out of these foodstuffs for a long period of time and still there was no Master Wu. The jacket I made for him was already finished, and I myself had tried it on a couple of times. It was very comfortable, it was warm.

One day Ah Liu saw me wearing that jacket and she couldn't hold back from asking, 'Master Wu hasn't come to see us for a long time. We don't know why, he was never like this in the past. This jacket has been ready for quite some time, all it needs now are his buttons.'

'Ah Liu, don't let the others know that this jacket is for Master Wu, because he may never come back.'

'I say he will definitely come back. As long as Old Master Tang isn't back, he won't abandon us.'

'How do you know this?'

'He told us, Uncle Ding was there too. He said he wouldn't ever abandon us. He's also collecting rent for Old Master Tang's fields. The young masters and misses' school fees are being paid with the rent money.'

'Ah Liu, promise me you won't let the children know about this jacket. You must never mention it, not even in the future.'

'I won't, you don't have to worry about this.'

That day I had to bring a pile of costume designs to the costume supplier. I walked to the railway station and was about to go through the gantry when someone called my name. It was Master Wu. I didn't know I would run into him there.

'Fengci, let's go for a meal. I just rushed here from Guangzhou, there's something I need to discuss with you.'

We chose the cleanest restaurant. After he ordered the food, Master Wu looked at me.

'Why have you lost weight?'

'Why haven't you come to see us?'

'I chose to stay away. What's the difference if I had come?'

When he finished speaking, he stared at me. I felt a twinge in my heart. After some time, I spoke.

'The jacket has been ready for a long time now, all it needs are the jade buttons. Come and collect it some time!'

'The jade buttons are here with me. Take them with you, sew them onto the jacket, and I'll come to get the jacket in two days' time, after I sort out some things.'

He took out a box from his bag. There were six jade butterflies inside. I took them from him and made sure I kept them properly.

'You said you had something to discuss with me.'

'I plan to move my family and business here, to Hong Kong. People say it's better than Guangzhou. I also want to let the boys have a western education. It'll give them better prospects in the future.'

'When are you planning to move here?'

'In two months or so. I've already bought a property in Hong Kong, our fields and warehouse have been sold. Now there's only the big house to take care of.'

'Old Master Tang asked you to collect the rental on his fields. Who have you asked to take over?'

'You will need to decide now. For half a year now I've not heard from Old Master Tang. Has he written to you all? Anyway, it's not much use waiting for his letters. Those fields are worth a bit, since you're not going into farming, why don't you sell them and move the funds to Hong Kong? You could buy a house or a yacht or a fishing boat to rent to fishermen. You would get much more than what you're getting now from that measly rent.'

I decided to sell those fields in Guangzhou's Zhujiang district. I decided not to wait for news from Old Master Tang.

After two days, Master Wu really did come to visit us. When Ah Liu saw him, she was so happy she shouted for me to come see. Thankfully the children were away in school.

I showed him the jacket. I stood behind his slight figure, and the urge to stroke the smooth fabric came naturally to me then. He suddenly turned around to face me and he put his arms around me.

I could have resisted, but it was useless, because this was also what I had been hoping for, for a long time.

5.

Master Wu sold our fields and brought the proceeds to the stone house. The two elder boys, Borong and Zhonghao, were at home. They were both twenty years old. Master Wu spoke to them, 'With this sum of money, you can buy three fishing boats. You can rent them out, you'll make quite a bit from that. Borong, didn't you say you wished to change jobs? You could take care of this boat rental business.'

'Uncle Wu's idea sounds good, but I don't know where to begin.'

'First you will need to register for a license. Only then can you start a business. Those fishing boats will require certification by a shipping service company. You mustn't be sloppy about such things. I just remembered, you're not even twenty-one! You're underage.'

'I am. It should be fine.'

'It'll take some time to get the license. Zhonghao, you should also quit your job. The two of you can work together on this. You could also look into other possible areas of business, for instance, getting cargo moved onto the ferries, or moving cargo from shipping vessels to land. There should be plenty of opportunities to make money here in Hong Kong as long as you're willing to work hard.'

'All that sounds really good.'

'Don't be happy too soon. The two of you are so young, there will be many senior and established folks at the Typhoon Shelter whom you will need to be properly introduced to. Be patient. I suggest you learn how to drive a boat first, and next you should also learn how to make your own repairs. After I move to Hong Kong, I'll introduce you to some people in the Typhoon Shelter.'

Our two young masters were glad to have him as their mentor. They became more cheerful, and began to speak and joke a lot more with me and their younger siblings. Our lives certainly improved.

In 1930, just as we had discovered a new means of making a living, Old Master Tang surprised us all by returning. He arranged for us to move to Nanyang with him, to Singapore, where he had started a tea wholesale business and bought a large house on River Valley Road. In a flash, we would have to leave Hong Kong and relocate to Singapore.

This seemed very unfair to all of us. These few years I had struggled to make ends meet in Hong Kong and just when things were about to improve, just when the children had made friends and gotten settled in their schools, just when the two young masters were about to start their own business, we were told to pack up and move.

Borong and Zhonghao had just started their fishing boat rental business and they refused to move to Singapore. The three of them argued heatedly over this.

I had just received a new order for costumes from the supplier, so I couldn't accompany Old Master Tang to Singapore. He returned on his own. I had to promise him that I would join him with the children in the autumn.

After Old Master Tang left, Master Wu came to look for me.

'Have you decided what you're going to do? Are you going to join him over there?'

I couldn't give him an answer.

'If you stay here, I'll look after you.'

'I don't need you to take care of me, I'm doing very well by myself.'

'This means you've decided to stay.'

'I've not decided yet, but I did promise Old Master Tang that I'll bring his children over there, so that they can be reunited.'

'If you go this time, I worry that it'll be hard for us to meet again.'

'So what if I stay here? You have your wife and concubine, you have your sons and daughters. Why would I tussle with them over you? What happened to Small South Strong remains deeply imprinted in my memory. Just before she died, she said she wished to turn into the yellow jasmine flower. Why should I bring trouble upon myself?'

'If this is what you want, there's nothing for me to say.'

After Master Wu left in a fit of anger, the children returned from school, they called me Ma, they told me what happened today in school, they recounted what they observed on the streets. How could I give these children up? In Singapore I would live with Old Master Tang, and he would have me as his only companion, our lives would be simpler than before.

Once I made up my mind, all I had to do was to wait for the coming of autumn. Master Wu learnt of my decision. He continued to pay us frequent visits but he didn't speak as much to me as before.

Borong and Zhonghao would stay in Hong Kong to grow their fishing boat rental business and Master Wu promised to look after them.

On the day of our departure, it was early autumn, and when we boarded the ship at dusk, it felt chilly. Master Wu accompanied us on board, he said goodbye to me on the deck.

'Last night I was thinking, since you'll be in Nanyang, there's a good chance that I'll come over too and when I'm there, I'll definitely look you up. By then Old Master Tang would have passed away, my wife and concubine would be old, the two of us can become companions who chat about the past. I've spent time these past weeks reflecting, and I've come to accept that it's possible to love someone quietly. Since you know how I feel about you, this can be enough.'

I had nothing to say to that. He took off his jacket with the jade butterflies and draped it over my shoulders: 'Take this!'

He left after that, his head bowed down. With his jacket on my body, I felt as warm as if he was embracing me. Unwittingly, my tears began like the rain.

The foghorn sounded, the ship began to move. I was deeply upset. After I stood up to look back towards the dock, I did not see him, I saw only the white waves of the ship's wake, and I felt myself being sent away on the ship's body, sent away!

Epilogue

In the autumn of 1980, it was Little Grandmother's eightieth birthday bash. At four o'clock sharp in the afternoon, the six of us girl cousins arranged to meet at the famous antique shop De Bao Zhai. We were planning to buy her a Longquan celadon piece for her birthday.

We were working adults by then, and we took care with our clothes and accessories, so when it came to what present to buy for our grandmother, we were of course very particular.

De Bao Zhai was renowned for its collection of Chinese carvings and ceramics. It was the best place to buy premium pieces of Longquan celadon, Liling porcelain, Yixing celadon and Jianshui pottery. The young owner's surname was Wu, his ancestors were in the Cohong of Guangzhou. He was known for being ethical in his business. The ancient traditional wares in De Bao Zhai were of the best quality, and their designs were unique too. These aspects attracted us to the shop, which seemed to fit our requirements.

'What do you ladies wish to look at?'

'We want to buy a Longquan celadon piece.'

'That's hard to come by!'

'It's fine, just show us the pieces you have.'

The aquamarine glaze of Longquan celadon is delicate and glossy. The most prized pieces are a pale green, and Little Grandmother would love a piece of this celadon.

The owner showed us vases. They were simple and elegant. They seemed both sturdy and fragile. The veins in the glaze had crab claw patterns or frost patterns or Chinese dodder patterns and so on. Although they were high quality celadon ware, we weren't happy with them.

'Do you have anything that's more refined and has an unusual design?'

'Let me take a look at the back. There should be one or two that are more unique. Please wait for a short while.'

We browsed the displays in the shop whilst he went to the back of the shop. Shortly he returned with two pieces of celadon. An old man who looked like he might be eighty years old came with him. Though old, he was clearly in good health, which might explain why he was wearing a traditional Chinese jacket made of cotton. His trousers were made of the same material.

We were busy looking at these two new pieces of celadon, so we didn't pay the old man much attention.

One of the pieces was a vase with wavy lips. That was its distinctive feature, those lips. The glaze was a jade-like green, and in its gentle and lustrous quality, it also resembled ice.

The other piece was a green eggshell porcelain bowl. It was exquisitely translucent.

The six of us began to discuss which one we should get. Some of us preferred the vase, some of us preferred the bowl.

'The vase is good. When Grandma is bored, she can touch it.'

'Yes! On the first and fifteenth of the lunar month, she can put chrysanthemum flowers in the vase. White or yellow chrysanthemums would look good in it. The kind of chrysanthemum with those dancing petals would look especially fey and dashing in this vase.'

'Even without flowers, this plum-green colour is such a pleasure to look at, Grandma will surely love to look at it.'

'The colour is truly beautiful, it's so delicate and soft, Grandma will love it.'

We were making quite a lot of noise. The old man who was standing there asked us, 'How old is your Grandma?'

'Eighty. Today is her eightieth birthday celebration.'

'The vase would be a better present for someone who is elderly. I personally chose this vase, it is one of a kind. I wasn't intending to sell it, because I like it a lot! See how the green makes it look like jade. These days they don't make glazes like this anymore.'

The old man came close to us. Suddenly the expression on his face turned. With trembling fingers, he gestured at our jade butterfly pendants.

These ten years, every time we visited our Grandma, we wore our jade butterflies, and today, since it was her big birthday celebration, of course we didn't forget. We noticed how agitated the old man was, and we had no idea why. He was stuttering.

'You, these jade buttons, jade buttons, where did you get them?'

'Our Grandma gave them to us.'

'They were originally a set of buttons.'

'Grandma removed them from a traditional Chinese jacket.'

'The jacket became too worn, but the buttons were still fine, so Grandma had them made into pendants for us. It's been ten years.'

Suddenly, one of us exclaimed, 'The jacket! Did that jacket belong to you?'

Silence all around us.

We were quiet for a long time until one of us asked, 'May we know your name?'

'My name is Wu Yu. "Yu" means jade, as you know.'

'Our names are Xun Ru, Cai Ru, Xuan Ru, Pu Ru, Jun Ru, Wan Ru. The Chinese characters of our names all contain the character "yu" for jade. Grandma gave us our names.'

'Grandma's favourite colour is green, jade-green!'

'How long has it been since you last saw each other?' we asked him.

'Forty, fifty years.'

'Oh! Half a century.'

'Quick, quick, let's go look for Grandma, what do you say?'

'Yes, yes, let's go now.'

Everyone in De Bao Zhai crowded around us to see what the commotion was about, to hear our story. When everything had become clear, the old man said, 'Good, good, let us go now. Let me go change my clothes.'

He went to the back of the shop, we paid for the vase, and waited impatiently for him to reappear.

He came out in an indigo jacket with white cuffs at the sleeves. There were six butterfly buttons on his jacket and they were also made of jade, except they were a much deeper green than our jade butterflies. His trousers were white. They complemented his snow-white hair. We were in our twenties and we had never seen such a well-dressed and distinguished-looking elderly gentleman before.

He strode towards the store entrance. We followed him in a single file. The manager called after him.

'Father! Are you going to a birthday celebration without a present?'

Old Master Wu waved his hands, gesturing to his son that his presence would be the best present of all!

Ah! Those jade butterflies, those jade buttons, they were like spirits, drawing this relationship, which had spanned half a century, to a satisfying conclusion.

From then on, we named the jade of those butterflies 'spirit-buttons of jade.'

THE SONG OF LIFE

Everybody expected Sister Margaret to scold me and dole out a severe punishment. She was speaking in English and in a loud voice: '… she is our student, she is one of us. If we don't love her, who will love her? If we don't help her, who will help her?'

I stood silently on the stage. I was a pitiful sight. I lowered my eyes to gaze at the bump that protruded from my school uniform…

Every day at five in the evening, I took the tram through the central district, heading for the eastern parts. The tram moved along its cable, like life being pulled ahead by time. Time cannot throw life aside, because the fact that life has growth proves that time exists. Erosion and the wear and tear of things over time is also proof that time is passing. This is true of all life forms, plants and animals alike. It's also true of inanimate objects: stone, earth, houses, chairs – nothing is spared the ravages of time. And it is also through time that the worth of things is validated.

For a pregnant woman, going through the tram gantry and climbing up to the carriage on the upper deck might seem difficult, but I was young and stubborn, and I wanted the view of the streets from the upper deck. I liked that feeling of looking down from above. And especially more so on that day. With night time approaching, the street lights were coming on, and to sit on the tram's upper level, looking out at the lights… just seeing the neon lights from right to left, up and down – it was uplifting.

Lots of people were out and about, coming out from office buildings, stores, walking on the streets, crossing the roads; they were like ants, rushing to and fro, anxious to go home. I always liked to sit in the last row, where I could look into the heart of the streets, where I could see the crowds scurrying around like insects, where I could see the lights changing. Once it was dark, I would be home.

My mum simply couldn't stand the fact that I went all around town with my bump. She scolded me, but she still cooked for me, made soup for me, so I never answered back; I was grateful for the double-boiled chicken and beef soups she made especially for me. Were there any parents in the world who never had reason to scold their children? Furthermore, I had committed such a grave mistake, I had brought shame to her. Even if she were to feed me pig slops, I would make myself swallow the lot. She was into tough love, the kind of mother who was harsh with her tongue but still cared about me.

My dad wouldn't be home till ten, because he taught at night school. He had taken on two jobs because we needed the money. He always brought snacks home for me, either zhaliang or spring onion pancake. He often bent over to speak to me at my desk.

'Don't stay up too late. Studies are important but so is rest.'

I didn't have anything else to do except study. The other advantage of studying was that I could close the door to my room and my mother would have to stop nagging, and I couldn't hear her telling my dad all my faults within earshot. When my mum got really angry, she would also scold my dad.

I felt like I couldn't continue living at home, especially after giving birth. I didn't want my baby to live in a home where there was so much scolding going on. I needed to find my own life, but I had no means to do so. I went to see Sister Margaret, and I spoke honestly to her about my needs.

'I want to work in an orphanage. I want to bring my kid up in an orphanage.'

'Can't you live at home?'

'My mum scolds me all the time. She's deeply unhappy with me, it's hard for me to live there.'

'We don't have the funds to hire a full-time teacher.'

'I don't need to be paid. I just want to live at the orphanage with my baby.'

Sister Margaret looked into my eyes and said, 'Because of you, I will be stepping down as principal next year. The church will send me to manage an orphanage. Perhaps we could run a kindergarten there that's open to the public. There should be demand for it since parents these days are paying more attention to early education for their children.'

I would forever be indebted to Sister Margaret.

Not too long ago, I stood on a beach facing the South Pacific Ocean. The sand was as fine as powder, the night breeze was warm. I was waiting for a sea turtle to come to the shore. It didn't notice me, it was determinedly and clumsily crawling some distance away from me, where it started to dig a hole that was large enough for it to lie inside and be buried. Once its body was covered by sand, it began to lay its eggs. I went near it, I saw the painful expression on its face as it closed its eyes. There were tears but no sound from the creature, not even a moan. Once it had laid its eggs, it crawled out of the pit, covered the eggs with sand, and slowly crawled towards the sea. I patted its back, as a way of wishing it well on its sea voyage, and looking towards the east, I saw the dawn beginning to break. The turtle swam towards the light.

At that moment, I seemed to understand what life was about, so I didn't go back to the hut where I had been staying. I went directly to the small town, where I boarded the first bus to return to the city.

I attended one of the city's top schools, an all-girls' mission school. The principal was a nun called Sister Margaret. She was known for being stern and having high expectations of us, not only in our academic results but also in our character and values. When I realised I was pregnant, Sister Margaret was the first person I told. I had been prepared for a slap and punishment; my plan was to kneel down and beg her to take me in, to let me stay in the orphanage behind the school.

It was close to evening that day. The light in the chapel was dim. In that small space I felt the judgement of the world breathing down on me. I was the worst person on earth! I knew that whatever happened next, it would be all my fault.

Sister Margaret walked towards me. The expression on her face was deadly serious, as if what she was going to say to me would bring down upon me a great force of condemnation. At that moment I became conscious that I was no longer just a teenage schoolgirl, I carried another life inside my body. I stood before her and watched as she raised her hand, anticipating the next movement of that hand, that it would most likely be delivering a painful slap to my face.

But that didn't happen. Sister Margaret drew me close to her and embraced me.

'I will do my best to help you and to protect you,' she said in her usual steady tone. That night, I stayed in the convent and during the night the baby kicked inside me. Perhaps that was when I knew that I would go home the next day after school.

There was school assembly in the morning. After the Lord's Prayer was said, Sister Margaret asked me to go on stage. The whole school was there, all one thousand and five hundred students. Many of them stared at me. Some looked anxious and frightened, some reminded me of the sort of people who would gather to witness an execution. Word had gone round about my situation. I was sure that running through the minds of every student and teacher present that day was the thought: *Now she's in for it.* I myself expected nothing short of the harshest possible words or punishment, or even the possibility that Sister Margaret would expel me. When Sister Margaret spoke, a hush fell across the hall.

'This student is with child. Most people will not forgive her for what she has done. She has committed a huge error, she had made a big mistake, and she should be asked to leave the school, although the church doesn't have any rules on this. Now I wish to ask all of you to consider one thing: she is our student, she is one of us. If we don't love her, who will love her? If we don't help her, who will help her?'

I was silent on that stage. I stood up there with my head lowered and looked down at my bump. I imagined that at any moment the others were going to rush onto the stage to kick and hit me, to hurl abuse at me. I imagined they would kick me out of the school gates and tell me never to show my face here again. There was no telling what people would do to protect the reputation of the school.

Miss Kong, a teacher whom I had always respected, stood up to speak.

'If this student is allowed to remain in the school, other students might think that her actions are acceptable. What happens if there are more cases like this? I hope that the principal and my fellow teachers will agree with me that this is a highly severe matter and should not be dealt with lightly.'

Miss Zeng spoke in her usual gentle tone of voice.

'I feel that we should give the student a second chance. She is a child herself and already she has to worry about taking care of a baby. Her example will serve as a warning to other students. You will all have to consider carefully whether you want to make the same choices that she has made, because look at the consequences!'

Miss Cheng also addressed the school. Apart from Sister Margaret, she was the teacher most of us feared because she was strict and fierce.

'This tells us that there's an even greater problem than the plight of one student. It's an island-wide problem, a national problem. We should work with the Ministry of Education to fix this problem. We should look towards America and Europe where sex education is part of the curriculum.'

Everyone in the hall started talking at once. What did Miss Cheng mean? What was sex education?

Sister Margaret took the microphone: 'Dear teachers and

students, I would like to hear your views. I would like to know if you feel that this student should be allowed to remain in school for the two months running up to the Cambridge "O" Level exams, or if she should be asked to leave. She would have to move to the orphanage as her parents would not let her stay at home. Many of you know that she'd been absent the past two months. Her parents had sent her to Nansha Bay. She pleaded with them to let her come back because she would like to finish her studies and sit for the exams. Now that you've heard her story, if you are against my decision to let her stay in our school, raise your hand.'

Three teachers' hands shot up. Some students raised their hands initially. But in the end, only the three teachers' hands stayed up. I saw all this from the stage. I couldn't help it. The tears just started.

After assembly ended, some of my classmates came to touch my bump, their eyes filled with excitement, curiosity, fear, pity. Near us, the teachers who had raised their hands were speaking heatedly with Sister Margaret. The teachers would then hold an emergency meeting.

After school, I went home. My parents were both civil servants. They were ashamed of me. My mother had been the first to realise that something was wrong. She interrogated me first. Next, my father grabbed me and demanded to know who the man was. After they found out it was someone they knew, that he was a good friend of my dad's, my mother hit me. I didn't fight back, I knew I was in the wrong. I was also shocked by the changes to my body. My breasts were swollen, the bump was beginning to show, I was feeling ill every day. Soon it would be impossible to conceal the facts. My parents decided to send me to Nansha Bay. After the child was born, it would be given away. Abortion was never an option because it was illegal back then, and we were Roman Catholics.

That day after the school I confronted my parents.

'I want to come home!'

'I want to face you, I want to face our neighbours.'

'I want to go back to school, I want to make it to university.'

'I want to keep my child, I want to watch my child grow up.'

'I love you. Please love me too!'

My mother said:

'If I had known you would turn out like this, I would have strangled you when you were born.'

'How am I going to show my face to our relatives, our neighbours?'

'How can I go back to work?'

'Why did I give birth to a slut like you? It's all your father's fault, he and his no-good friends.'

My father said:

'Come home!'

'After your "O" Levels, after you've given birth, go look for a job. As for university, we'll figure it out later.'

'Your mother doesn't have to go back to work. She can hide at home!'

'Don't move to the convent. Sister Margaret rang me earlier on. She reminded me, if we don't protect you, who's going to protect you? She reminded me that I have to be a good father to you.'

And so I had to endure the curious looks of our neighbours when I moved back home. I put up with their curious looks by greeting them and chatting with them. I wasn't like this before, I used to be arrogant and aloof, but after I moved back, I made an effort to be friendly and polite. After a while, no one pointed their finger when they saw me, they didn't make a big fuss anymore, the only thing they did was to warn their daughters not to be like me.

Later on, I heard that the three teachers who raised their hands at assembly resigned because of me. One of them wrote an article about the school's decision which was published in the newspaper and caused a furore for a while. The school lost its standing in the eyes of the public. I was very upset by that of course, but what could I do? I couldn't do anything so I kept myself busy by focusing on my studies.

When I was sent to the hospital to deliver my baby, it was half eleven at night. The last time I saw a gynecologist was to have my pregnancy confirmed. Because of this, the hospital staff were thrown off when I showed up. The administrators, nurses, and doctors bombarded me with questions:

'What? You've not had any pre-natal check-ups since your second trimester? No one has examined you the past four months, do you know how dangerous that is?'

'It must be illegitimate.'

'Aiyah! She's only fifteen!'

'Look at you, so skinny and your tummy so big, cannot, what, never been checked by a doctor, so who's going to bear the responsibility now?'

'Who's the baby's father? What? No father?'

'Oh, this must be your dad and mum!'

By now my mother was already sobbing. I told my father, 'Please take her home, and call Sister Margaret. She will know what to do.'

My mother had grown faint from crying, so my father had no choice but to send her home. He said he would be back. After they left, I sat on the bench and looked at the mouths of the receptionist, nurses, doctors, all those strangers who didn't know anything about me, and their mouths were spewing judgement and accusation. I touched my belly and begged the new life inside, *Please come out of there as soon as you can! I can't take any more of this, so don't take your time, just come out of there!*

The contractions began almost immediately. It was an unbearable pain, the sort of pain that had me pleading for it to stop because it was so overwhelming. I forgot that I was still in the hospital foyer, sitting before the registration counter. I was in so much agony I screamed and screamed and no one could make me stop.

The director of the hospital finally arrived. So did the head of gynecology. I wasn't sure what it was that they wanted to say or do to me, I only knew that the contractions were killing me, and I put all the anger, frustration, all the emotions I'd had to repress over these nine months into my cries.

Finally, I was put on a bed.

Finally, I heard the gentle voice of a doctor, who said, 'Don't be afraid, the difficult part will soon be over.'

I was determined to take a good look at him. He sounded so confident, so kind. I saw an Indian man with large, bulging eyes. I burst out laughing. How could such an unattractive person have such a soothing voice?

'Good girl, you're laughing. What's the reason?'

'I feel happy inside!' I uttered in between the contractions.

'You're really a good girl. Come, it's time. Push!'

It'd been such a long time since anyone called me a good girl. Moreover, it was entirely justified; I was no longer a good girl. Yet from time to time, he urged me in English, 'Push harder! That's right! What a good girl!'

Under this shower of praise, I gave birth to my daughter. She weighed seven pounds and eleven ounces. The doctor said to the nurse, 'It must have been difficult for such a small person to have carried such a heavy infant.'

'She's only fifteen!'

The doctor put his hand on my sweaty brow.

'After going through labour, is there anything else to fear from life?'

The nurses were silent, but I would carry his words with me forever. In life, you would always know who loved you and who didn't care about you. The people who loved you weren't just the ones who were related to you.

Sister Margaret was the second person to carry my baby. She said to the baby, 'My sweetheart, how much trouble you've caused! Ai! But I see your big black eyes looking back at me and what can I say, except that it was all worth it! Truly worth it!'

Later I named my baby Gracie. I breastfed her. It was an absolutely intimate connection.

Whilst she suckled at my breast, I felt my vagina shrinking. I could feel the pain there though it was slight. My breasts changed from being engorged to being relaxed. The mother's sexual organs and her body are inextricable from life.

Over time, the baby grew bigger, and in the night, I often breastfed her and read. Because I was engrossed in my reading, I wouldn't notice that she had already had her fill. She looked at me with her round black eyes until I felt the pressure of her gaze, and I would put my book down. She must have wondered why it was that her mother liked to read so much. From then on, my daughter, books and I would co-exist on the same plane.

Three months later, the 'O' Level results came out. I obtained seven distinctions. Miss Zeng wrote to the papers about my results, citing me as an example of a lost sheep that was rescued.

At the start of the following school year, the Department of Education announced that sex education would be introduced to all schools through a series of talks and film screenings and other relevant channels of information. They also made a new ruling that pregnant students would have to go on leave of absence for a year, that they shouldn't be allowed to go back to school until they had given birth.

So I count myself as being blessed. At that time, in that kind of environment, I was lucky not to have been driven to jump into the sea. To persevere at life, to meet my circumstances with courage. This was the lesson I had gleaned from the sea turtles. Life is so precious, and it comes with such great responsibility. I heard that the turtles would return to the beach where they had laid their eggs during the hatching season. Whether the baby turtles were theirs or not, they would shepherd them, guide them, to return to the sea.

BLOSSOMS OF THE MOON SEASON

Prologue

NO OTHER FLOWER has a bloom like the Chinese Rose. Its name is Yueji; 'yue' for 'moon', 'ji' for 'season'. She is in bloom from May to November in northern China, and in Jiangnan down south, all year long. Her other names – Yueyuehong (Everlasting Red) and Changchunhua (Flower of Eternal Spring) – also pay tribute to her resilient radiance.

Unlike the peony, her beauty isn't showy. Nor does she possess the elegance and classical beauty of the cherry blossom. But she holds her own among these prized flowers by being in bloom through the year, undaunted by changing seasons and the ravages of time.

She flowers for every moon, month after month, for which she has been praised in verse: 'A blossom falls, another one appears in its place, unfazed by spring's arrival and departure.'

In the north, the south, or the South Seas; during autumn and summer; under blazing sun, interminable rain, or starlit skies on balmy nights – this is a flower which doesn't waver, always living life to the fullest, giving herself and her beauty unreservedly. For this reason, many succumb to her charms. As the saying goes, 'No one under the heavens can resist the beauty of the rose in flower every season.'

1.

Yueji and Yongquan have been together for a decade. Like any couple, they have had their fair share of fights but nothing has angered Yueji as much as their row this time, which is why she has threatened to leave him.

Yongquan had asked her to chip in 30,000 dollars for the lease of a retail unit to start a music shop at Queenstown Shopping Centre. 30,000 dollars was her life savings. Because she was too trusting and naive, she thought that her name would be on the lease agreement. Instead, he put his wife Fengying's name on the agreement. Yueji was furious, how could she accept this? She felt she had been scammed and used. She lost respect for herself. The incident showed, in her view, that between her and Fengying, Yongquan cared more for Fengying than her, and this was what she found most unbearable, that the ten years with him had been for nothing.

She flung herself onto the bed and lay there with her bankbook open on the last page where the last withdrawn figure of $30,000 was clearly printed. She bit her lower lip, her heart was in great pain, she blamed herself for the mistake. She sprung up from her bed and went around her flat assembling the objects that Yongquan had bought for her over the past ten years and lugging them outside to the corridor: the TV set, video cassette player, microwave oven, pots, pans, a leather armchair, videotapes, his clothes.

Her fourteen-year-old daughter, Xiaojia, was shocked to tears, and she cried out: 'Mum, Mum, don't be angry, no matter what he's done, Father loves us.'

'He's not your father, you and your brothers are not to call him that anymore. He's not your father by blood, he didn't raise you, why should you call him Father? Who does he think he is?'

'Mum, don't be angry, please stop throwing our things outside.'

Their neighbours heard the commotion. From doorways and

windows they peeked at what was going on. No one intervened.

Just then her son, the one who was in NS, came back and saw the mess on the corridor outside their flat, and after he pried the truth out of her, he advised his mother:

'Mum, for these ten years you've not minded that he didn't marry you, why should you begrudge him now?'

'You have no idea how much money he's taken from me all these years! He's been helping himself, bit by bit, to the insurance money your father left for us, until there's hardly any of it left!'

'He's been like a father to us, paying our school fees, buying books and clothes for us, taking us out.'

'Are you saying that I've done nothing for you? I slog at my sewing machine day and night. It's bad enough that you have no sympathy for me, you're even taking his side.'

'Mum, don't be angry, let's go back inside. We're not defending him. Surely you can't deny that he's been good to us these ten years, that he's been taking care of us; when we were little, if anyone hurt us, bullied us, he would stand up for us, he would go after them. When Xiaojia had high fever, he was the one who rushed her to the hospital. He's loved us as if we were his children. I know of fathers, my friends' fathers, who haven't shown as much love to their own children.'

'That was when you were all little. Now that you're all grown up, I don't have to put up with him anymore.'

'Mum, why are you punishing yourself? Come, let's move our things back inside.'

'Don't you dare! If you touch them, I'll leave.'

Her sons behaved as if she'd not said anything and moved all the things back inside. She couldn't bear to watch them, so she went downstairs and walked towards the street from Tiong Bahru towards Outram, she walked until it grew dark. She found herself standing outside a matchmaking agency in midtown. Perhaps she was still distraught, whatever it was, something made her decide to push the glass door and walk in. A middle-aged man greeted her and introduced himself as Mr Luo.

'Am I too old to register?' Yueji blurted out.

Mr Luo scrutinised the woman before him:

Petite, and clearly middle-aged; she was slim and she didn't have a tummy. Although she was dressed simply in a top with a Chinese collar and matching slacks, her clothes were well cut, showing off her womanly and trim figure.

This woman was different from most of the men and women who'd walked through these doors over the years. Her looks were plain, but when she spoke her eyes shone with intelligence. Her eyebrows were thick and bold. The dark circles under her eyes and the fatigue in her aura and her every gesture – these were flaws, but they were not insurmountable.

'How old are you? Were you married before?'

'Forty-two. I was married, then my husband passed away. I have three children.'

'Three?'

Mr Luo was thinking, this is going to be tough. Widows are not popular, and being saddled with three children takes away all remaining hope. Seeing that hopeful brightness in her eyes, he decided, perhaps something could be done for her. Anyway it wouldn't hurt to try. He took a form from one of the drawers and gave it to her.

'Can you write? Good, fill this up, make sure you put down everything that's relevant.'

Her handwriting was neat and attractive. She probably attended secondary school. In her self-description she wrote:

I was widowed at thirty. I have three children: two sons, twenty and eighteen, both in National Service; the youngest is fourteen, she's in Secondary Two. I work as a seamstress, I make suits and cheongsams.

For her hobbies, she wrote: *I like pop music. I enjoy watching Hong Kong TV dramas. I don't drink, I don't gamble.*

'Your Chinese is pretty good.'

'I grew up in a nunnery. The nuns taught me how to read and write.'

'Don't you have any family of your own?'

She shook her head.

A wave of pity rose in Mr Luo. He said quickly, 'Once I have news of someone suitable, I'll call you.'

The moment Yueji stepped out of the agency, her heart felt lighter. She wasn't in the mood to return home yet, so she crossed at the lights and walked to Haisan Street where she saw a fortune teller. She went over to his stall. If she had her fortune read by him, she could find out when her luck was going to change.

The man had a huge birthmark on his temple. He squinted at her through his bifocals and asked for her birthdate and time of birth. All the while his hands trembled. He frowned as he studied her face.

'You lost a large sum of money recently.'

Ah, how could he possible know about that! Her heart began to race.

'Is there any way I can get it back?'

'No. The money was given to someone you love. Unless you break off the relationship, your fortune won't change.'

'And if I don't? If I stay with him?'

'I can't say for sure right now. The knot that binds you to him is very tight for now, it seems that it can't be loosened.'

A shadow crossed over his features. The fortune teller picked up her hand and examined the lines on her palm. The life line was pointing at the food line's peak, suggesting that she was predestined to be wealthy; a fine line could be discerned by the side, tiny but distinct, and this signified that she had a benefactor. The fortune teller looked up.

'The money you lost recently is not that big a deal. Soon you will have manifold riches, many times what you'd lost! In future you will own a lot of land, meadows and fields, just you wait!'

The fortune teller's voice dwindled into mumbling, it wasn't possible to make out what he was saying. Yueji was stunned into silence. The locksmith at the neighbouring stall said, 'You've had your money's worth. I've never seen him say so much to anyone before.'

Yueji took the hint and paid the fortune teller eight dollars. She turned over what he'd just said to her over in her head: *Just my luck! He's clearly not right in the head. Where do we have land here in Singapore for me to own? Meadows and fields? It's hard to find even a vegetable farm here!*

As she walked along the street, she could see that all the shops were closed. It was time to go home. She got on a bus and made her way back to Tiong Bahru.

2.

At home she found her children waiting up for her, together with Yongquan. He rushed up to her side.

'Please forgive me. I'm in a difficult position. As you know, she's had high blood pressure all these years, and now she has diabetes too. I feel responsible for that. Maybe her poor health is caused by us. I've always felt guilty. Besides, the video tape company that folded, it had been under her name, so I felt it made sense to put her name down for the cassette shop.'

'Why did you ask me to invest in it? You should have asked her.'

'She has no money, I'm sure you know that. I'm broke too. If you didn't agree to help me, I wouldn't have been able to start this new business. I can work for other people, I am not afraid of hard work, I don't have a problem with that.'

'Good! Why didn't you say all this before you accepted my money? I'm so dumb, I thought since I'd given you some money, you would definitely include me in the business, I never thought you would treat me in this way! I've ended up not only helping you but helping her too. How can you expect me to be alright with this?'

'You're making the situation sound much worse than what it is. The children are here, please watch how you speak. I've already told you that I'll be giving you revenue from the sales. Your shop is close by, you'll be able to see for yourself how well the business is doing, how can I keep anything from you? Her name is just a formality, you'll be getting a cut of the money!'

'I won't be so lucky. Seeing the stall makes me so mad I wish it'll quickly fold.'

Yongquan, who was calm up to this moment, became enraged by her words.

'How can you curse me? The stall hasn't even opened yet and you're wishing that it'll fold!'

Yueji's children shook their heads and interjected:

'Mum, why did you say that? If the stall folds, you'll lose your money. Uncle, don't be angry. Both of you need to calm down.'

'Stop arguing, the two of you! Aren't you hungry? Let's all go out for supper!'

That night Yueji couldn't sleep. Yongquan went back to Fengying's place. Yueji couldn't stop turning over her head the fortune teller's prediction that it would be tough for her to end this relationship.

She was thirty-three when they met. She'd been widowed for two years and she was lonely. Yongquan and some friends got together to open an electrical goods store at Queenstown Shopping Centre. It was the largest retail space in the mall, occupying three units, and it sold all sorts of appliances, of great range and variety, from refrigerators to computer games. She got to know Yongquan and his partners well, and if visitors wished to have drinks, her sons went to get them. They also distributed the store's flyers at the housing estate, or else they played computer games at the entrance to drum up business.

That was how her sons became attached to Yongquan.

One morning after she had sent her daughter to kindergarten, she was making her way to a bus stop when a small truck stopped before her. It was Yongquan. He told her to get in, and when she hesitated and tried to come up with an excuse, he said loudly, 'Get in quick, there's a bus behind us!'

She got into his truck. He was a married man, this was the reason for her reluctance.

Yongquan gazed at her. There was emotion in his look. Yueji was usually reticent, she buried herself in work at the shop, busying herself with making clothes, and when she was away from the sewing machine it would be to get her sons to have lunch or dinner. She had the air of someone who had been abandoned by the world, when in fact she deserved to be loved, taken care of, supported. Yongquan often noticed her in the store, and there were many times when he wished to touch her, hug her, but he always held back.

He was annoyed at himself. He pressed the button for the car stereo with more force than was needed and the song that started playing was one he liked: 'Where does the Wind Come From'. He paid attention to the lyrics:

Fall in love if that's what you want, love if you wish to love, no one can tell me, where the wind is from, it comes and it goes...

What an adorable song!

Fall in love if that's what you want, love if you wish to love...

Yueji gazed at Yongquan, she could sense what was on his mind. His lips were pressed tightly together, giving his face an irate expression. Who was he mad at? Her heart fluttered. Ever since her husband passed away, she'd not loved anyone, her heart was closed. He had liver cancer, discovered at a late stage. The diagnosis took them by surprise, and she was rendered helpless. They saw western and traditional Chinese physicians – if someone was recommended to them, they went to see the doctor – but in the end nothing could save him.

They were a loving couple. He was a taxi driver, she a seamstress, and their sons were good boys. When the youngest was four, she'd told her husband she would like to have a daughter, but she couldn't have any more children, so they adopted a baby girl, Xiaojia. When her husband fell ill, Xiaojia was only one. As he drew his dying breath, he stared hard at Yueji, his eyes filled with longing and sadness.

Yueji realised that Yongquan's car was not going towards Queenstown. It was on the Pan-Island Expressway. She didn't say anything.

She didn't mind him. During the lunch and dinner hours when there were fewer customers in his shop, he helped her sons prepare for their English spelling tests. If they scored well, he bought them ice cream. He was very indulgent towards them. She warned her sons not to take advantage of Uncle Quan and they shrugged, telling her that she need not worry, Uncle Quan was different.

She was too bogged down by her own worries to rein them in.

The car was driving towards Punggol Beach. She'd not been here in ages. In the morning the sea was peaceful, and she gazed at it, feeling a peace she had never had before come over her.

'Let's go for a stroll,' Yongquan said.

She got out and they walked on the sand, keeping a certain gap between their bodies. It was nice, walking together like this, and Yueji was glad. After they had been walking for quite some time, Yongquan suddenly said, 'Let me carry you.'

Yueji was stunned. She felt lightheaded and then Yongquan held her hands, crouched down, and carried her up easily on his back. Yueji wrapped her arms around his shoulders and felt his strength as he ran a few paces and slowed down. She was moved, she pressed her face into his back and she started to cry. His shirt became damp but he carried on walking. He didn't stop walking as her tears grew louder, and this intensified her emotions until her entire body started to tremble.

It was only then that he stopped and he pulled her down to face him and he kissed her on the lips. She didn't stop him, she only cried, as if to let out all the unhappiness, frustration, loneliness of these past years. Yongquan carried on kissing her, caressing her, and he made her lie down on the beach with him. With sand as their pillow and the sky as their blanket, they made love and became free.

3.

In the days that followed, Yongquan often came to her place for dinner. He also took her children to the movies and the swimming pool. He didn't conceal how he felt about Yueji, not even at the shopping centre. It wasn't long before everyone there, the shopkeepers and regulars, knew about his affair with Yueji. The news reached his wife Fengying.

One day Fengying came to Yueji's shop. It was around eleven in the morning. Yueji thought that the woman in front of her was a customer. The woman had a plastic bag with her and Yueji greeted her with a smile. The woman untied the bag, releasing a putrid stench. Before Yueji could step back, she was drenched from head to foot in pigswill.

Yueji realised what this was about. Yongquan and some people rushed over. Yongquan grabbed hold of Fengying who kept shrieking at the top of her voice, 'Slut, bitch, adulteress, whore…'

Yongquan dragged her out of the shop and made her go home with him. The bad smell wafted everywhere, which made everyone hold their noses and curse, many complained loudly whilst others fled the building.

Yueji held back her tears. She changed out of the stained clothes in the washroom and brought several buckets of water to clean the shop floor. Despite her efforts it still stank. She ignored it, gritted her teeth, sat at the sewing machine and worked furiously. Her feet never left the pedal. Tears began to roll down her face, like a flood through sluice gates, they kept on flowing. She paid no attention to them, she let them dampen her blouse. A crowd gathered outside her shop. They watched and talked, no one came to comfort her, not a single one. At one something her sons came to the shop after school and they asked her, 'Why is it so smelly, mum? It's so smelly.'

'Are you crying, mum? Did someone bully you?

Yueji didn't say a word. She stood up, got her sons to gather their school bags, shuttered and locked the shop, and strode out.

Her sons trailed behind her.

'Mum, where are we going?'

'To fetch your sister.'

'After that where are we going?'

'We're going to have a feast and then we're going to watch a movie.'

'Really?'

Xiaojia was over the moon when she saw them; Yueji usually didn't collect her till seven in the evening, but today she was so early, the children at the childcare centre hadn't even taken their afternoon nap. As Yueji reached for her daughter's hand, the little girl said, 'Smelly mummy!'

Yueji ignored her. From behind she heard her younger son whisper to his brother, 'Mum is really very smelly.'

'Keep quiet, if mum gets mad she won't take us out for a big meal and a film, just put up with it!'

It would be hard to find sons and daughters who didn't have to put up with their parents all their lives, and putting up with them actually means being flexible and adaptable.

Yueji paid no attention to her children as they followed her, suffering in silence. She brought them to a western restaurant because her sons liked western food, and she bought them each an ice cream. They were so happy with these treats that they forgot about the stench. They caught a movie screening at four, it was *The Private Eyes*, a Hong Kong comedy by the Hui brothers about the woes of ordinary people, and it was so good it made Yueji forget her troubles and she laughed so hard she cried.

After the movie they went home. It was already seven. Her children sprinted out of the lift ahead of her, racing each other to their door. Ahead of her she could hear her sons' speaking loudly:

'Uncle Quan, Uncle Quan, why are you sleeping here?'

'Uncle Quan, we went to see a really good movie.'

'Uncle Quan, did you have too much to drink?'

When Yueji reached her doorstep, she saw Yongquan in a drunken stupor on the floor. She was angry and she would have walked past him into the flat if he had not been woken up by the children's loud voices and found her right in front of him.

He cried out, 'Don't ignore me, say something!'

Yueji stared at him, she opened the door with her key and the children squirmed past her to get inside, she too dashed in, and swiftly closed the metal grille door. Yongquan staggered to his feet and stuck his hand into the wooden door jamb to stop her from closing it, shouting after her.

'Let me in, Ji, listen to me, let me explain, I've made it clear to her, she won't cause trouble for you anymore, listen to me, open the door. Xiaohua, open the door, Xiaoguang, open the door, let me in, I've brought you a new electronic game, quick, let me in.'

Xiaojia, who was at the doorway, ran to her mum.

'Mum, give Uncle the key to the grille.'

'No, and if any of you dares to let him in, I'll break your legs.'

She turned her back on them, went to her room, and closed the door. In the living room the front door was still open.

Her three children knelt behind the grille.

On the other side, Yongquan begged them to unlock it.

Neighbours came to see what was going on. Yongquan said the children's mother had gone out and taken the key with her. The neighbours responded, 'Well, then you'll just have to wait for her to come back.'

Shortly after that, Yueji came out of her room and yelled at the children to do their homework. She spoke coldly to Yongquan.

'Go back, we're finished. I have three kids to take care of, so stop bothering me. For that alone I'd thank you.'

'Listen to me, she really won't cause any more trouble for you. She's also aware that the culprit is me, and I gave her my word, that I will never divorce her, I will always take care of her, our daughter's school fees, I'll be responsible, I'm not the sort of man who's not responsible.

'She wants me to quit the electrical store, she wants me to do something different, I've also given in to her. Anyway, there are too many partners in that business, I wasn't making a lot of money, so I've decided I'll start a new venture.'

'That's good. We won't see each other anymore. It'll be a clean break.'

'Yueji, I beg of you please, let's not break up, let me visit you, take the kids out, you know my daughter's already eighteen and in JC, she can't be bothered with me anymore, but your children are still young. I can help you take care of them, lessen your burden.'

'Yongquan, I can't accept your offer and I'm perfectly capable of taking care of them myself, please go!'

'Alright, I'll go, but only if you're not angry at me.'

After Yongquan left, Yueji heaved a sigh. She felt exhausted, truly exhausted, exhausted in a way that was new to her, so that life, her past, her future, the status of her relationship with Yongquan, everything felt like a burden to her, a bother. But she couldn't leave them, she couldn't shirk her responsibilities.

The children thoughtfully went to bed without resistance, even the four-year-old Xiaojia had climbed into bed without changing out of her clothes. Xiaojia's eyelashes were long, resting on her sweet pale face. Her daughter, the poor child, teased at her tender age by Yongquan, who would get her to call him 'Father' before he would give her a toy, and she didn't care, she did as she was told, which made Yongquan very happy. He would carry her, swing her high up towards the sky, and whatever she asked for she would receive from him. If Yongquan were to become her father, at her tiny age she would have had three fathers: the one who'd made her with his seed, the one who'd adopted her, and Yongquan who loved her. Yueji thought, why was life so tiresome? It felt as if the gods were making fun of her!

She went back to her room, realised she hadn't showered, her whole body stank and she should give herself a thorough wash from head to toe. She bathed carefully, and she did it over and over, using a lot of shampoo, a lot of soap, washing herself until she was satisfied. It was only when she was finished that she saw that the towel was not on the rail. She stepped out and walked to the wardrobe, her body naked and glossy, and there before the wardrobe mirror she looked at herself, at the shining drops of water. She liked what she saw, she loved that her skin was still fresh, that her body had not lost its beauty, she loved her body as much as her life.

With her hair tied up she looked much younger than someone in her thirties. She looked at her eyes and her eyebrows, she saw how the eyes smiled, and how striking her brows looked without make-up. They were thick and dark, suggesting that their owner was someone very headstrong.

She told her reflection in the mirror, *Live well, live for your children, for yourself, for life, do whatever it takes to survive.*

That night she slept very well. She was filled with confidence and self-belief.

4.

The next day, Yueji went to her shop at the usual time of nine in the morning. The janitors had already mopped the floors of the whole building. On her level, they'd sprayed a strong disinfectant, it had a sickly-sweet scent. She laughed bitterly. The air in the shop still bore more than a hint of the awful putrid odour of pigswill, so she took out the air freshener she'd brought with her and walked all around the shop spraying it.

People are adept at hiding things. It didn't take much to take care of foul smelling air.

There was no one else around, she was the earliest. This was something that the nuns had taught her when she was little:

'We must always be earlier than the devotees. They should arrive to find us already in the temple hall, joss sticks in hand. As they come in, we should go up to them and offer the incense to them. It's the same with everything else in life, no matter what the occasion is, if you're early, you will have had time to prepare your heart and mind for whatever it is that you mean to attain. You would be in a stronger position.'

Yueji got down to work. After ten o'clock, the neighbouring shops started to open. The others saw that she was already there. Yueji was so hardworking, nobody had the heart to speak ill about her. And they had their own problems to take care of, their own businesses to tend to. Yueji kept to herself, she wasn't a gossip, she didn't go around the other shops, she kept her head down and worked; they all knew this about her, and this was another reason why they left her alone.

Yongquan on the other hand started to keep a much lower profile. He used to go around to the other shops, he was very friendly and got on well with the other retailers, and often joined them for coffee and chitchat. He was easy going, generous and warm. His wife's attack on Yueji made him lose face. He became self-conscious about what people could be saying about him.

Not long afterwards, he sold his stake and invested the money in a video rental company at Bukit Ho Swee. The business flourished.

He still went to Yueji's. At first she ignored him, but her children adored him, especially her two sons, and they often went out with him. Yueji punished them harshly by caning them. Her younger son yelled at her.

'Why can't we hang out with Uncle Quan? If you don't want to be with him, that's your business. We can still be his friend.'

She screamed at them, 'If you want to be with him, pack your things and go, don't come back and don't call me Mum!'

She didn't expect him to put his clothes into a carrier bag. She gave him two tight slaps. He gave her a vehement look and she started to cry. Her eleven-year-old son's voice was breaking, he was becoming a stranger to her, she had no idea how to speak to him, he wasn't like her elder son Xiaohua, the sweet-tempered and obedient Xiaohua.

They continued to fight until Yongquan arrived and Xiaohua let him in. He coaxed the boy, putting his hand on his shoulder, reasoning with him. Yueji could hear her son's voice, the uneven sound of that half-boy half-man voice, through her tears.

'She's getting stranger every day, unreasonable, always angry, and when she's angry she scolds us. She doesn't allow us to do this, doesn't allow us to do that, she's like a kangaroo stuffing us in her pocket.'

'Ha ha, Xiaoguang, your mother's not a kangaroo, she loves you, everything she does comes out of concern for all of you. That's why she's worried about who you are with.'

'What's wrong with us being with you? She used to go out with you too, now she's fallen out with you, she wants us to kick you out of our lives, that's so unreasonable, and anyway she was the one who told me to leave…' the boy blubbered.

'Your mother would never ask you to leave, she was just speaking out of anger, she didn't mean it. You are a good boy, you are doing great in school, why would your mother ask you to go away? How could she bear to lose you? It's my fault, I'll speak to your mother, I'll ask her to get back together with me. Once that happens, you won't get any more of her scoldings!'

Yueji gave in to Yongquan after that. She was too tired for one, and she could see that her sons needed a father, so she bowed her head and let Yongquan back into her life.

Her life continued to be a trial, for both she and Yongquan had terrible tempers, and so they often squabbled, and their fights were only resolved when both sides agreed at the same time to give way. The children grew up in this volatile environment; there was as much sun as there was rain.

Ten years went by. They were years of happiness and togetherness as much as they were years of unhappiness and disunity.

The rising popularity of videotapes created a problem: the widespread piracy of videos imported from Hong Kong and Europe. The government clamped down on companies that offered such services, and cracked down on video rental stores with pornographic and violent movies in their video libraries. Those who were prosecuted had their licenses revoked.

Yongquan did not realise how serious the situation was. He was also a careless man by nature, and he wasn't aware of how the tide had turned. Whilst others in the same industry were busy getting rid of videos that might get them into trouble, he didn't do a thing until it was too late – his company was forced to suspend its operations and its license was revoked.

It was a huge blow to him. He lost a lot of weight, he became a ghost of a man, aimless and lost. He changed: from someone who knew all the material comforts of a good and easy life, who had many friends and a very active social life, he became a loner who stayed at home all day, reading the newspapers. There wasn't that much to read anyway, not enough to keep him occupied beyond the morning.

Yueji felt sorry for him. So when Yongquan said he would like to start a new business venture, she decided to support him in every way possible.

At that time her older son was due to complete his National Service in a few weeks, her younger son had just started his Basic Military Training, and her daughter Xiaojia was in Secondary Two.

Her late husband was a prudent man who had bought insurance policies for the children to take care of their education needs. Because she didn't have to worry about the children, Yueji decided she would use her savings to invest in Yongquan's new company.

What she didn't expect was that Yongquan would put his wife Fengying's name on the deed and not hers, that he would put Fengying's feelings ahead of hers. It seemed that he was more afraid of making Fengying angry than of making Yueji upset.

As Yueji lay on her bed, fuming over all that had happened these ten years between them, she felt her heart turn cold. She was seized by the desire to cry and yet she felt too that it wasn't possible for her to cry, even though deep inside she felt an extreme pain and hurt and disappointment.

5.

Yongquan's new shop was in Queenstown shopping centre. Many of the shopowners there who knew him from before came to congratulate him. Fengying was also at the shop on their first day of business, and she greeted the guests. Yueji didn't go to her shop or to Yongquan's shop. She worked from home that day, using the sewing machine in her flat. She thought about things he said to her:

'Fengying said she'd like to work at the cash register, she doesn't mind that your shop is close by. Because you've helped us by investing your savings into the business, she's grateful, she can see that you're sincere about helping us.'

Yueji smiled bitterly. Did Yongquan think he could have his cake and eat it too? She was glad she had had the foresight to hire an assistant who could take care of the shop for her whilst she worked from home. She didn't have to go to the shopping centre and face Fengying. Her neighbours came to her to get clothes made or altered, she had enough business, she didn't have to go back to the shop.

By then, she had been thinking of leaving him for almost a year. She was already forty-three, what was the point in being with him when she didn't see a future for them? Without him, she could be happy. She had her kids. Her eldest son had a girlfriend, and in a few years' time she'll be a grandmother, busy and happy with her grandchildren. What more could she ask for?

She was deep in thought when the telephone rang. It was a stranger's voice. He said he was Mr Luo from the matchmaking agency.

'I have a customer with me. He lives in Hong Kong. His surname is Zeng. He would like to meet you. He's sixty-one years old, he's a businessman. He's the first one to express interest in meeting you since you registered with us a year ago. It's a rare opportunity.'

'I'm not interested.'

'You can't back out just like that. This was what we agreed on when you signed up. Look, what's wrong with coming to meet him? It's just a simple introduction, take it as an opportunity to make a new friend. Nothing wrong with that. Will you come? We'll be waiting at the agency.'

After Yueji put down the receiver, she didn't get ready immediately. She sprawled on her bed, nestling her cheek onto the soft blanket. She was very comfortable there, she didn't have to go; they would give up after a while, they would know she wasn't going to show up.

But she also felt curious about the sixty-one-year-old man from Hong Kong. Who was he and why was he interested in her? Was he a manual labourer? Did he have pockmarked skin? Or was he fat, squat and old?

She got up and went to her wardrobe. She chose a celadon green top with small embroidered white flowers and polyester wide-legged trousers. She applied an orange-red lipstick. It was too bright, she blotted it with tissue and added a layer of lip gloss. She brushed her hair, put on a pair of colourful wedges, and was soon on her way to the appointment.

She considered taking a taxi. She took the bus instead. What was the rush?

When she reached the agency, she could tell that Mr Luo had

been anxiously waiting for her to show up. There was a man with him: tall, genteel, over fifty, wearing glasses and dressed neatly in a brown striped shirt and beige trousers.

Mr Luo introduced them.

'This is Mr Zeng. He's from Hong Kong, and he's interested in finding someone he can settle down with. He spent the whole morning going through our files. You're the only one he's interested in meeting.'

'Madam Yueji's surname on the form is Hua. Are you the descendent of Hua Mulan?'

'No, I grew up in a Buddhist nunnery, I don't know who my parents are, and the nuns said that the people who came to pray always brought flowers, so they gave me Hua as my surname, and then for my name they thought they'd choose a specific type of flower. At that time there was a vase of Yueji flowers in the main hall. They named me after those flowers.'

'What an interesting story.'

'What about you, what's your name?'

'Zeng Tianfu.'

'Destinies can be changed by names. You are going to be blessed indeed!'

'Is that so? You're quite superstitious, aren't you?'

'I've always had my fortune read. Does that count? My life's not been easy, seeing the fortune teller is a source of consolation. I'm hoping that my luck will change for the better.'

'What matters most is that we rely on what we've been given, and we do our best.'

'I don't disagree. I've been making a living as a seamstress, that's how I raised my children. My sons are doing their National Service, my daughter will be taking her "O" Level exams at the end of the year.'

'You look young for someone who has grown-up kids.'

'I'm almost forty-four. You look young for your age too. On the phone Mr Luo mentioned that you're sixty-one.'

Mr Luo took this mention of his name as an opportunity to interject: 'I'm glad to see the two of you getting on so well.'

'It's thanks to you, Mr Luo. Let me take us all out for dinner tonight. Mr Luo, you're included too.'

'Why don't the two of you go ahead? I will join you another time.'

Over dinner Yueji put her shyness aside and asked Zeng Tianfu, 'There are many good women in Hong Kong. Why didn't you search there?'

'I did try over there, I went on a number of blind dates set up by matchmaking agencies, but none of them worked out. I'm not a talkative person, if the other person doesn't speak, I find it hard to start a conversation. The women in Hong Kong find me dull.'

'You're too modest, Mr Zeng. I'm not very talkative myself. Talking can be quite tiring sometimes.'

'Do you really think so?'

'Yes, I prefer to work, or to listen to Cantonese opera, or music, or go out and window shop or just walk around the city.'

'I'm the same! I like to walk around in the city, not to get anything done or buy anything, just to look at people, and what's going on outside. That's what I like to do.'

'When I'm not in a good mood, I take the double-decker bus, and I go up to the second level, I find a window seat, and I look out at the signboards, the people getting off work, the daylight growing dim as the day ends, the street lamps turning on, the neon lights...'

'Yueji, that's the sort of thing that I do too. My wife passed away three years ago, and my son and daughter both left for the US, so there have been times when I didn't know what to do with myself, and I go out and I ride a bus all around Hong Kong Island. I can see the sea, and the ferry lights at night, the bright lights of Kowloon across the water. You should come to Hong Kong sometime, I'll show you around.'

'I've not really travelled. The furthest I've been is Hat Yai in Thailand. I went there by coach, I've never taken a plane.'

'Would you like to visit Hong Kong?'

'Yes. But it'll have to be at the end of the year, after my daughter's exams. I'll come and look for you then, would that be alright?'

'Of course!'

They ate in silence after that, both of them deep in thought.

Yueji was thinking: *Mr Zeng was the exact opposite of Yongquan in his temperament, but quite similar to me.*

Mr Zeng was thinking: *I guess she's not really interested in me, she seems to think that my invitation to her is for her to come and be a tourist in Hong Kong when what I meant is that I'd like her to live with me. I'll have to speak to Mr Luo tomorrow.*

After dinner he sent Yueji home and they exchanged addresses and telephone numbers.

Yueji felt relaxed and contented at home. Yongquan didn't come over, and she didn't mind.

She didn't think too much about having a future with Mr Zeng. To her he was a new friend, someone she could speak to and write letters to.

6.

The following day, Mr Zeng rang her in the afternoon and asked her out for tea. He needed to speak to her, he said. When they met, he told her, 'I didn't come to Singapore to look for a wife. I was walking around and I came across Mr Luo's agency. I went inside and Mr Luo told me about you. After I read your form, I thought I'd like to meet you. When you came to the agency that day, I liked you, because you are sincere and down-to-earth. Most middle-aged women put on airs. There's a simplicity about you which I find very attractive. You are independent and sensitive, these are qualities which I admire. I'm wondering if you would be interested in moving to Hong Kong.'

'Mr Zeng, there are things you don't know about me. I've been in a relationship for some time, it's just that in the past two years things have not been good...'

She began to tell him about Yongquan, how they met, how Yongquan had pursued her, how she was humiliated by Fengying, how she'd trusted Yongquan with her savings. She told him everything.

Mr Zeng shook his head and sighed from time to time. When Yueji started to cry he gave her his handkerchief but he didn't stop her from speaking. He listened intently to everything she said. It was dark outside by the time she finished.

'It sounds like your relationship with that man is no longer what it used to be, there may not be much point in letting it drag on. I'm not saying this for my own interest in the matter, but from an objective point of view, as someone who's listened to what you've shared.'

'I know. I'm also aware that it's pointless to cling onto that relationship. In the end I'll be the one who suffers and I'll resent him even more for it.'

'You should leave him and give yourself time to heal. Spend time alone, enjoy some peace and quiet. I can be patient and I'm willing to wait and see how our feelings stand a year and a half from now.'

Yueji agreed with him. Even if Mr Zeng had not come into her life, her affinity with Yongquan had run its course. It was time to end the relationship.

A few days later, Mr Zeng returned to Hong Kong.

Business was good at the new shop, which kept Yongquan busy, and he didn't see as much of Yueji. It was also harder for him to see her as Fengying was at the shop every day.

One day, Yueji invited him to her place for lunch, to let him know that she wished to break up with him.

Yueji cooked pig stomach soup, his favourite. She also prepared steamed pork with cuttlefish, panfried sand goby fish, and spinach stir fried with oyster sauce.

Yongquan tucked in happily, telling her how well the shop was doing, and how in less than two years they should earn profits. Yueji thought he was going to return her savings to her, but he didn't bring up the 30,000 dollars she had lent to him. Instead, he talked about opening a second outlet. Yueji felt disappointed.

Forget it, break up with him! Do it now, break up with him! The voice inside her mind was firm. Finally, she spoke up:

'Quan, I'm breaking up with you.'

'What?'

'I'm breaking up with you!'

'Why?'

'Because I don't want to be the third party anymore. Besides both of you are much closer these days, if I cling onto you, things could go horribly wrong for all of us. This is how crimes of passion happen. I have a hot temper, and your wife is even worse than me. It's really not easy for you to be caught between us. Let's break up now whilst everyone is still calm and rational. You can continue to keep yourself busy at the shop, it'll be a distraction for you. As for me, I'll let someone else take over my shop, I've been doing quite well with my neighbours as my customers, it's actually more than I need. Xiaohua and Xiaoguang are already young men and Xiaojia will be in JC next year. I can put my feet up now, they're all grown up.'

'Yueji, I'll never leave you.'

'Listen to me, I'm going to tell you the truth now: I met someone. His surname is Zeng, he wants to marry me.'

'Who are you talking about? Who's this man?'

Yueji told him how she met Zeng Tianfu.

Yongquan didn't say anything for a long time. Yueji gazed at him. He was weeping. Weeping like someone who had lost everything.

He wasn't this upset when his last business was forced to close down.

Yueji could feel his sadness. Tears streamed from her eyes.

'If this is what you want, I won't get in your way. But I want you to find out more about that man, be certain of his character.'

'I'm not in a rush to be with him. I just want to give myself a chance to experience life differently. I may or may not get together with him in future. It's not yet been decided.'

'You'll definitely join him, I can sense it, you're going to abandon me!'

He broke down into tears.

When a woman is jilted by a man, she becomes a figure of pity. When a man is jilted by a woman, he is even more pitiful!

Yueji finally left Yongquan, and her shop unit was let out to someone else. What caught her by surprise was the phone call she received from Fengying.

'Why did you break up with him? I didn't interfere with your affair all these years, and now he's all depressed at home. He told me everything.'

'Is that so? Well, it can't be helped!' Yueji replied. She told Fengying she had to go out soon. It wasn't true but she had no interest in letting the conversation continue.

After hanging up, she couldn't help smiling. What was the world coming to?

She wrote a long letter to Mr Zeng, letting him know everything that happened between her and Yongquan. She wrote about how she felt. She was surprised by her trust in him. What mattered to her was not whether she was going to spend the rest of her life with Mr Zeng in Hong Kong, but his friendship and their heart-and-soul connection.

Mr Zeng wrote back soon after that. He proposed to Yueji in the letter, and attached an air ticket for her to fly to Hong Kong.

After Xiaojia completed her exams, Yueji flew to Hong Kong. She told her three children about Mr Zeng before she left.

Her eldest son and Xiaojia had no objections, only the younger son spoke up:

'When we were in secondary school, we knew that you and Uncle Quan were together and we knew that it wasn't right, but we couldn't stop you. Now you've finally thought it through and left him, shouldn't you spend some time alone, enjoy your hard-won peace? Instead you've gone and found yourself another man, this Mr Zeng. Mum, don't you think this is all too fast?'

'I'm not like the three of you, time is on your side. Your mother is almost forty-five. How many more years will I have? Mr Zeng isn't like Uncle Quan, he's retired, he's a widower, his son and daughter are in America. He's all alone, and like me, he just wants to find someone he can spend time with, a friend and companion to enjoy the remaining years in peace.'

'Since this is what you want, then I have nothing more to say. Mr Zeng's marriage proposal shows that he's serious about you. In fact, you and Father didn't go through the civil ceremony, so when you and Mr Zeng get married, it'll be your first true marriage and we will attend the ceremony, we will come to give you both our blessing!'

At that moment Yueji realised her children were truly grown up. All her emotions uncoiled and loosened, she could feel an overwhelming and unprecedented sense of release.

After she reached Hong Kong, Mr Zeng shared with her his dreams for their future life together:

'I would like us to move to Zhongshan in China. I have a house and some land over there. After I sell that land to developers, we will have sufficient money to live well in retirement. Tomorrow we will go to the lawyer's and have a will drawn up. Should anything happen to me, you will be provided for. There will be nothing for you to worry about.'

Yueji was stunned. She remembered the fortune teller's words: 'You will be wealthy, you will own land.' Back then, she had dismissed his prediction as nonsense, not for one moment did she consider that he spoke the truth.

Mr Zeng waited for her to say something. When she remained silent, he went on, 'I have savings and some shares. I will give some of these to you, so that you feel secure.'

'No, no, enough, enough!' When she agreed to marry him, she

had no idea how much wealth he had.

Mr Zeng smiled:

'Who on earth would say no to more money?'

'What we have in life is predestined. I saw a fortune teller who told me that after years of not having very much and not much support from anyone, my luck would turn. What I have now is more than enough for me, I'm very grateful and contented.'

Mr Zeng gazed at her in wonder and drew her close to him. To meet someone like Yueji in his sixties was truly something he hadn't expected. His heart swelled with happiness.

Epilogue

Yueji married Mr Zeng on the tenth day of the tenth month of the lunar year at the Singapore Registry of Marriages. Mr Luo was Mr Zeng's witness and I was Yueji's witness. You may ask, what's my connection to Yueji? I'm one of her customers, I've had many clothes made by her, including the lovely Thai silk cheongsam I wore at my wedding.

After she got married, Yueji lived in Zhongshan, a Chinese city in Guangdong province. I asked her how she liked her life over there, she said:

'After morning exercise, I eat breakfast, listen to Cantonese opera, chat with Mr Zeng about our plan for the day, then it's lunchtime, followed by a nap, and after that we visit friends and play chess or chat. In the evening we go out for a stroll, and usually dinner is at a late hour, after which I'll spend time with Mr Zeng, chatting, and while I watch television, he'll read or do research. This is usually what happens each day.

'I don't have to do housework, we have two helpers, an elderly woman and the other one who is younger. One of them prepares our meals, the other one does all the housework. I lead a comfortable life, there's nothing for me to worry about.'

Life is unpredictable. She had gone through so much, and yet before she left, I heard her saying to her daughter:

'Xiaojia, I'm not sure which is more accurate, to say that your life is tough or to say it isn't? If we say that your life isn't easy, how then did you come to have four fathers: one who gave you life, one who adopted you, one was your Uncle Quan, and now there is Mr Zeng.' Who could have expected her daughter to reply in an even more surprising way:

'Who cares about all that, since I've always thought of myself as someone with a mother. I will live with as much strength as my mother, I will shine like her!'

ABOUT THE AUTHOR

Soon Ai Ling is a native of Huiyang, Guangdong. She holds a bachelor degree in Chinese Language and Literature from Nanyang University, Singapore (1971), and a PhD in Philosophy from the University of Hong Kong (1995). Soon is an award-winning author of several novels and anthologies. Her works have been translated into Japanese, English and Malay. She was a lecturer at the Hong Kong Institute of Education (1997-2005) and Assistant Professor of NIE at Nanyang Technological University, Singapore (2006-2013). At present she is a guest lecturer at the Education University of Hong Kong and the Nanyang Technological University, Singapore.

ABOUT THE TRANSLATOR

YEO WEI WEI is a writer and translator based in Singapore. Her short stories have been longlisted in the Commonwealth Short Story Prize (2021) and Glimmer Train (2013). She holds a MA in Creative Writing (Prose Fiction) from the University of East Anglia.